DEDICATION AND QUOTES

For Tom

"Things go and things happen and you're there, I guess."
—Rob Machado

ACKNOWLEDGMENTS

My thanks and love to:

My husband and my children, for allowing me time to write and for not asking too many questions;

My brother, Nelson Wells, for understanding;

My parents, for not reading what I write;

Carol Sautter, for loyalty;

MAV, PM, and Laura Victoria Kline Bartels (my Marie), for literally saving my life in February 2014;

Blake Darrington, Joyce Lombard, and Linda Kottler, for guidance;

James R. Dobbins, Jr., for getting me past the wall;

Theresa Robledo, for flowers and for dishing, regularly;

Ari Larson, Dena Wyand, and Mary-Allyn Garcia, for believing that I was a writer when I didn't believe it myself;

Doodlebug, for the Grubmeister;

J.D. Hawkins, for inspiration and for listening to my stories;

Kristy Lin Billuni of www.sexygrammar.com, for getting me out of the writer's closet and for holding my hand;

Amanda Billuni, for the introduction and for a long, lovely history;

Kristen Vail, for reading my shit early;

Maxine Donner, for adding commas and for having my back, always;

BG Davies, for telling me that I didn't need commas;

Little Dude, for sexy giggles;

Catherine Bibby of Rochelle's Reviews, for taking a chance on me and for my first blog review;

Maria Monroe of Graffiti Fiction, for Hemingway;

Candi Kane of the Dirty Laundry Blog, for auto-correct fails;

Heather Lynne of Obsessed with Myshelf, for being my spirit animal;

Jen McCoy of the Literary Gossip, for my first shout out;

Jerica MacMillan, for editing assistance, although all errors are mine;

My beautiful family, colleagues, and friends, for love and friendship; and

The magnificent people in the Wattpad, Twitter, and Facebook reading and writing communities, for your support.

I love you all

THE SUN AND THE MOON

ONE

Not All Accountants Drive Harleys

HE PANTED OVER ME, sweat beading on his forehead, his veins straining in his neck. I grasped his smooth, naked back, and then his ass, while he thrusted into me. I faked a moan and kissed his ear. He groaned loudly. I let go and ran my hands through his soft, light brown hair.

I just wasn't into this. I'd a better chance of getting an orgasm in the NARS aisle at Sephora. There, an "orgasm" was a certainty, after I handed over my credit card for an overpriced powdered blush, in a pinky-peach color, called ORGASM. Here, it was a crapshoot. But I'd decided to try it tonight, after putting him off for three months, hoping that it'd be worth it. He was really sweet at dinner. It was a good dinner. The champagne was nice. I thought the sex would be good.

It wasn't. Goddamn it. Goddamn him. Goddamn me. Goddamn

the antidepressants. *I was entitled to an orgasm.* But the pills made it hard for me to come. I didn't think it was impossible, though. Dr. Google and Dr. WebMD said it could happen. So now I was pissed and blaming him and me for not doing this well, but I decided to hide my anger with a gasp, which he interpreted, incorrectly, as something like pleasure or enthusiasm.

So he gripped my ass, and thrusted faster and harder. Harder was okay with me, but it didn't hit the right spots. And I wasn't sure that I could guide him to the right spots if he asked. I made the decision, then, to just get this over with. Not only the sex but also the relationship. It was a relationship with a little "r" anyway, not a big "R." I could kick him out right now, but that was kind of a shit maneuver. I mean, I invited him here to do this. I wanted to try it. This wasn't my first time in bed with a man. But right now, I didn't have the energy to talk with him and tell him what I wanted. I didn't want to explore. I didn't want to communicate. I just wanted to be over and done with this night.

My mind wandered. I was bored and distracted. I knew that I was supposed to be into it—all consumed, all lust and climaxing and shit like that. But no, as he moved, I looked at the ceiling of my 1927 Santa Barbara adobe, darkening in the dusky sky. I noticed patterns in the white plaster. The room was getting really dark. I never had sex in the full light because I didn't want any questions about my scars. Yet another reason why I put this off. I exhaled.

What's on TV later?

One of the channels was having a Harry Potter marathon.

I wish I'd gone to Hogwarts instead of law school.

Wait. Focus. Sex. We're having sex. I was doing it with Paul. He was cute and nice. He had lovely, soft skin and a shy smile. And he was an accountant.

Okay, so he was bad in bed.

Really bad.

Whoever said that sex was like pizza—even when it's bad, it's good—was a big fat liar. There was such a thing as bad sex. And bad pizza. I ought to know. I swear, if a man could make me orgasm—even if I had to break my Rules and do it myself—I'd stay with him for life.

At this point, I didn't think that I could turn this into good, or even slightly pleasant sex, nor did I want to. It was all my fault for being a closet romantic.

Don't ask me where I'd got it, but I had this impression that accountants were really bad boys who secretly rode Harleys on weekends, with, well, a naughty side, which would be unleashed once they got an erection. Not Paul. He was sweet, but not passionate. Kind, but socially and emotionally clueless. He seemed genuinely perplexed by me and my sense of humor. I'd caught him looking at me like he couldn't quite figure me out. He was good looking, but bland. Not particularly small, but not particularly big—in every way that you could imagine. He dressed well, but not flashy. He had a nice car, but not too nice. He listened. He was polite. He treated me nicely.

But there was no spark. My heart didn't beat harder when I saw him. I'd finally figured out that he wasn't hard to figure out: there was just no romantic, secret, passionate side to Paul the accountant.

The bottom line was, he liked taxes. Well, he liked figuring out how to get away with legally not paying taxes, and telling me about it in intricate detail. That was his passion. Sex? Not so much. I'm a lawyer, and I love me a loophole, but give me a break.

I'd thought this through logically: he was a guy, so he must like sex, and getting him naked would allow me to find out how much he liked sex, and maybe get an orgasm that wasn't an expensive powdered blush. But now that I was experiencing the naked side of Paul, I'd found out that fucking wasn't his strong point.

Wait. I didn't "fuck." I "had sex." Or "made love." Or "got busy." I was too classy to fuck. It was against my Rules. Well, whatever. He was better at preparing 1040s.

But he was also safe. There was no chance of him finding out about my Rules and therefore breaking them, because he didn't question me when I asked to do it missionary. He just strapped on the condom and started thrusting. That was a relief.

I think.

In case you were wondering, these are my Rules:

1. No sex in the daylight. Or any type of light.

2. No masturbation.

3. No doggy style.

4. No oral sex.

5. No submission. I am always in control.

6. No toys.

7. No spending the night, so I never do the walk of shame. And no one spends the night at my place.

8. Nothing demeaning.

9. No dirty talk.

10. I don't call it "fucking." I only "make love."

And anal didn't even need to be on the list because it wasn't even a consideration. Not in my world.

Yeah. I really am a princess with a stick up my ass, and yeah, I know that sometimes I say one thing and then do another. Deal with it.

Paul maneuvered faster now. Bless him. He was trying. But nope. Television was better. The stars weren't aligning. I wasn't going to come. The Prozac still messed with me and apparently, it had stolen my orgasm.

I noted yet another pattern on the plastered ceiling, now barely visible in the fully darkened room.

And he was really moving. It wasn't painful or anything. I liked the guy. But he just wasn't doing it for me. Nope. So …

What was on TV?

Focus, girl, focus.

Better fake it to get it over with.

"Oh God. *Oh God.* Paul. *Paul!*" I clenched my vaginal muscles, took a big breath, and then let the air noisily out.

He thrusted, sped up, and then stilled, pumping a release into the too-big condom. After a bit, he hugged me, kissed my forehead and rolled over, tracing my arm with his fingertip.

Maybe he'd leave soon, and I could rewatch *Order of the Phoenix*.

Thank God that was over. He looked pleased, though. I'd have to let him down easy. Tomorrow.

THE NEXT AFTERNOON I MADE it to my weekly appointment.

"When do you feel sexy?" my therapist asked.

"Never."

"Never?"

I nodded. "I'm not supposed to feel sexy. I want to feel pretty. Or hot. But not sexy. And most of the time I just feel fat. There's this lump here, on my belly, that's just not going away." She ignored my attempt to body shame myself, and went straight to the point.

"We'll set aside the issue of whether you are 'supposed to' do anything or not do anything for now. But using your words, why do you think you're not supposed to feel sexy?"

"I don't know what I'm supposed to feel or not feel anymore," I snapped. "But yes, I'm not supposed to feel sexy."

Yes, I'm weird. My belief is completely at odds with marketing today. Nowadays, everything's sex; I'm supposed go around feeling sexy since I'm a modern, enlightened woman. And it's true: I'm no virgin. I want my orgasm.

But somehow along the way, like a lot of us, I'd come to believe that sex, pleasure, and feeling good were all wrong. I felt guilty about sex, even though that was embarrassing to admit at my age. I was raised Irish-Catholic and taught to believe that anything pleasurable was bad. I had also learned that a woman was not supposed to be openly sexual. When that belief was ingrained in you, it was hard to believe anything else. If it felt good, it must be bad.

Really, it's part of the stern, cultural tradition of prudish sexual morality in America. I could blame it on the Puritans. But since they've been fucking gone for centuries—at least the kind with buckled shoes—I wasn't sure who to blame for my personal pathological repression.

How do you reconcile the fact that we're sexual beings with our mixed up cultural norms? And how do you do it on a personal level?

I did it by establishing my Rules. I gave my body sex but only on limited conditions. It worked.

Sort of.

Okay, it didn't.

After my experiences the past year, I was seriously considering revising these Rules. Indeed, after my sessions with my therapist, I now thought that this was a key part of the cause of my depression: denying myself pleasure. The thing was, when I really thought about it, what was wrong with sex? It's natural, biological. I didn't want to get a disease, or get physically or emotionally hurt. But after wanting to have sex, but only under certain conditions, for so long, I couldn't help but feel that I needed to change something.

"It's okay to have that feeling, you know?" said my therapist with a smile. "You don't have to like sex."

"But I think I want to," I said in a quiet voice.

"Then let's try something. I'm going to give you some homework. Do a few things to make yourself feel sexy. Make a list and do it. Buy some incredible lingerie. Get a Brazilian. Buy a vibrator. Read a romance novel."

"I don't read trash."

"*The greatest way to turn on a woman is through her mind,*" my therapist said firmly. "I'll give you a list of books to check out. That's what e-readers are for—so you don't have to go to the store and deal with walking to the register holding a book with a half-naked man or woman on the cover. Look, I understand you may feel uncomfortable about this, but I can assure you that it's part of healthy sexuality. Just try it and be open."

Healthy sexuality. Now there was a concept. I was almost giggling with glee. What would happen if I tried it? After so much therapy, I had broken through so many barriers and allowed myself to get out of a very bad place. But this was the final frontier. Giving myself permission to enjoy sex, huh? That could be good.

It was funny how quickly I dropped my defenses about this. Thirty-one years old now, I had lost my virginity when I was eighteen. That was a long time of simultaneously wanting to have sex and feeling bad about it. But now that I'd thought about it logically, I really wanted to engage in pleasure. I bet my brain would feel so good with an orgasm. I was ready to dial in.

"*I'll do it*," I pledged.

TWO

Green Eyes and Blue

THE PACIFIC OCEAN SPARKLED TO my right in the September morning sunlight as I drove south from Santa Barbara, my home, to Ventura, where I was to be in court later that day. Not knowing traffic, I'd left early, brought a laptop and some files, and intended to work at a coffee shop until I needed to be in court. I'd checked Yelp, and planned on trying Southwinds Coffee, an indie shop that was highly recommended, and close to the courthouse. Frankly, with an ocean-side drive almost the whole way, this was one of the best commutes in the world, and I was glad to be out of the office and on to court for a pretrial hearing. My big trial was scheduled in a week; this was some procedural garbage that I had to get rid of before the first day of the proceedings.

I tried to keep my eyes on the road as I drove my black Mercedes convertible down Highway 101, but the ocean was really distracting. Chamber of Commerce weather, I called it—clear, blue sky, murky, but silvery, green-blue water, and the crash of waves. No fog. You could see the Channel Islands in the distance and pelicans flying low along the shore. I bet if you stopped and watched, you could see dolphins. With the window open a crack, I could smell the ocean salt and stink. I still loved it.

I wanted to put the top down on my car, but that would muss up my hair, and I had to stay put together for court. I wore semi-badass lawyer attire. Full badass meant a navy pinstriped suit, pearls, and heels. Yes, traditional, but you had to play the part, and the clothes were armor. Fucking power suits. They worked. Semi-badass, my uniform today, meant a pale blue suit, with red heels and gold hoop earrings. I still meant business. But I didn't need pinstripes today, not for this type of hearing.

My hair fell down past my shoulders, and was very dark brown, almost black, with a lot of wave. I knew that I was lucky that it didn't get frizzy, it just curled more the closer I got to the beach. Driving alongside the beach didn't count. I'd be fine today.

Not that you could tell that I ever went to the beach. I didn't look like a California beachy girl even though I was a native Californian. I didn't match the type. My skin appeared so pale, naturally, and I spent so much time inside writing on the computer, and reading law books—and Harry Potter—that you really couldn't tell that I ever went outside. I loved the beach, but I usually went there in the evening, walking along the shore, barefoot, picking up shells and sea glass. That wasn't the way to get your skin tan. Still, I'd accepted my pale skin and learned to endure the comments from people who couldn't understand that I grew up here.

My favorite body part, hands down, were my unusual eyes—they were almost violet they were so blue. If you squinted and dressed me up right, I sort of looked like Elizabeth Taylor—pale skin, violet eyes, and dark hair. I knew that I looked alright. Too bad it was just a package. I knew that the insides were still fucked up.

As I drove, I thought about the past year. It was amazing that I was noticing things like the ocean sparkle and stink, the pelicans, the crash of the waves, and the islands. Depression made you not notice things like that. It closed your world down and you didn't enjoy anything at all. It was just too hard to do anything. Think. Move. Appreciate. Breathe. Too hard to do any of that.

Not that long ago, I had been suicidal. Panicked, I had called my best friend when I realized that I was driving around trying to find a good railroad track to stop on. This scared me badly—an understatement—and, in tears, I admitted my dark thoughts to Marie. She helped me to get professional help, and the professional help made me realize that I suffered from depression, and that this was something that was treatable, but I needed to work on it.

So, for the past year, I worked on it. I took medicine and went to therapy and exercised and *tried hard*. I felt stable, but I still felt empty most of the time. It was like something massive was missing. I could drag my sorry ass out of bed most days, but I wasn't sure of the reason why I did so. I was grateful that I was no longer driving around looking for railroad tracks, but I wanted to *feel something*. Depression had robbed me of most feelings. The main thing that I felt these days was numb. Maybe with my new "healthy sexuality" homework, I'd start to feel more than that.

Looking out at the sparkle of the water and the white of the waves as I drove, I decided to just enjoy that moment of this nearly perfect morning. It was beautiful. I had a whole day ahead of me. It was going to be okay.

Actually, it was going to be better than okay. For the first time in a long time, I noticed my surroundings, not just going around trapped inside my head. Seeing the sunshine and the ocean, I realized that I was truly starting to feel better.

With the help of my friend Google Maps, I found Southwinds Coffee, and parked in the spacious parking lot in Ventura near the courthouse. The coffee shop had big windows with black trim and a nice vibe—comfy, hip, and not too pretentious. Upbeat music played, but not too loudly. Good coffee shop smells. There was also enough space to spread out with a laptop. I noticed a lot of people working in little alcoves, with handy plugs spaced in the baseboards all over the place. A nice touch.

I stepped in line and waited to order, juggling my purse and briefcase with my laptop and files, absorbed with checking my phone. I was trying to look busy and important. I meant, dammit, I *was* busy and important. That was why I needed to check Twitter.

As the line moved steadily forward, I looked up. It was almost my turn. I grabbed a yogurt out of the cold case and shoved my phone into my purse. I put the yogurt down on the counter, looked up to order, and locked eyes with the most stunning set of greens I'd ever seen.

Without meaning to, I held my breath, staring into these sunny, intense eyes. I noticed that the vibrant green was flecked with gold, and the irises were warm and inviting. The eyes smiled, and I could not help but notice that there was apparently a mouth on this face. The most lush, pouty lips that I had ever seen smiled along with the eyes.

"May I help you?" the lips asked in a husky, sexy, low voice. How had I not heard that voice while I was waiting in line?

Help me. Yes, please help me. What was I doing here? I forgot. I was mesmerized. My mental hard drive was also wiped of any rational thought. My brain shut down. Failed me. Damn brain. Green eyes. Pouty, smiley lips. Husky voice. Help me.

Help me!

My world quieted down and closed up. I couldn't hear the music of the coffee shop or the chatter behind me. I couldn't smell the good morning coffee shop smells. All I could do was stare.

The lips grew into an even bigger grin and I shook myself slightly, grinned reflexively, and noticed the man behind the eyes and lips.

Golden, surfer boy curls crowned a tan face. High cheekbones, a strong jaw—damn, a good jaw, and a smattering of freckles. And, Lord help me, dimples. Two.

Holy hell, he was gorgeous. And familiar. I got the feeling that I'd seen him before.

He'd been leaning over the counter at my height, but now he stood up, still smiling at me, at full height. Um, dimples. Brain still not working, only focused on dimples. Then I noticed that wow, he was really tall. And lean. His black Southwinds Coffee apron wrapped around his narrow hips. He wore a short sleeve button-down shirt in faded plaid over a white t-shirt and his biceps bulged. No immediate tattoos visible.

I'd never seen a more beautiful man in the flesh. Manflesh. Now there's a word.

"Anything besides the yogurt," he asked slowly, gently, as if there weren't twelve people behind me in line. His name tag said Ryan.

Recovering with a snap, I finally said, "Yes. A latte, please."

He smiled and pulled a cup out, writing on it. "Regular milk?"

"Nonfat." He checked the box.

"And a name?"

"Amelia," I breathed.

He is the sun, I thought. He had a massive gravitational pull. I couldn't help but be drawn in by those gold flecks in his intense, but smiling, eyes.

Giving himself a little shake, as if he was dazed, too, he wrote my name on the coffee cup and handed it to the barista.

How much time passed? Hours? Days? I wasn't sure. I'd lost all sense of time locked in his gaze. I couldn't believe I was actually thinking that romance novel shit, not that I read romance novels, but it was true. I lost myself in his beautiful eyes.

He added up my total on the cash register and I handed him my debit card and he swiped it. As I grasped the card, my fingers grazed his and I felt a pulse go through my body, lodging between my legs.

Holy hell.

That did not just happen. But apparently it did. I stuck the card haphazardly in my purse and waited as the receipt printed.

Time passed. People grew old and died. Planets were born from stardust.

He handed me the receipt and I realized that it was time for me to move. Too soon. I wanted an eternity with him and I didn't even know him.

The noise of the coffee shop came back to life and I became vaguely aware of the dozen people pressing in behind me, needing caffeine. I was also vaguely sorry for coming between them and it. Okay, not really. It was every man or woman for himself or herself as far as caffeine goes. I was just sorry to leave the Sun God. I ducked my head and grabbed my yogurt, walking to the opposite side of the huge espresso machine to wait for my coffee.

I glanced over at his profile while he waited on the next customer, his hips pressed into the counter. I couldn't help it. He was beautiful, gorgeous, handsome, a hunk. My thoughts were overwhelming: I was drawn to him like crazy and I wanted to lick him, suck him, caress him, feel him, and have him make me forget about NARS ORGASM blush. I'd never felt this sort of attraction to any other person.

I'd not felt feelings, real feelings, in a long while.

He stepped back to allow the cash drawer to open and then I saw it.

Under his apron. Unmistakable evidence of his arousal. Shit. He was hard. Instead of thinking that he's a perv, as would be my natural snark, I thought, "Git me some, *STAT.*"

I tried not to stare but I did it anyway, then looked away. I looked back. He adjusted himself and leaned up against the counter, once more. I looked away again, and kept looking away, until I couldn't help myself. I caught a glance after the barista handed me my latte.

Still beautiful.

I turned and picked a table, walking to an empty one in an alcove out of sight of the counter and Mr. Sun God. I set down my laptop, files, and purse, and sat. I breathed. I slumped back.

What the fuck just happened?

It took me a bit to recover. Finally, I opened up my laptop and started working. Although I did some real work while sipping my coffee, I couldn't help but sneak in a few searches.

According to the ultimate authority, Dr. Google, after three or four months, women who use antidepressants and have trouble finding an orgasm, may be able to do so again.

I'd been on antidepressants for a year. And only one inept man in my bed during that time. It was time to test the waters. Time to rescue my orgasm from the drugs. Or from wherever it had been hiding.

THREE

Happy Trail

I SOMEHOW MANAGED TO SURVIVE in the coffee shop for an hour or so, going through files, and actually getting some work done. I didn't believe it was possible with Ryan the Sun God there, but having picked a spot where his gravitational pull was not so strong, I found myself absorbed in my work.

It helped that the Yelp reviews were right. The coffee here was unbelievable. I was a caffeine addict and had sampled my fair share of the drink, but this stuff was quite simply the best that I'd ever had. It left every other coffee shop behind.

In my workaholic state, I hadn't noticed that the place had cleared up. I'd noticed pretty quickly, however, that Ryan was going around the tables, picking up dishes and cleaning with a white dishtowel, wiping off tables.

So I thought, maybe I'll wait for him to come to my table.

But then what would I do?

Checking the clock on my phone, I realized that I had a little over twenty minutes to get to the courthouse, which was only a few blocks away, so I decided to pack up. I slid my laptop into my briefcase, and put away my files. I packed them up neatly. Then I looked through them again to make sure that I had everything. Then I checked my phone. And Twitter. And my email.

Okay, so I stalled a little. I wanted to talk to him. Even though I figured that I would be stupidly mute in his presence again, I still could not help myself.

I knew that I should be a badass, confident woman, and go find him myself, not wait for him to come to me.

Yeah, I would get right on that. In another life.

While I was busy trying not to hyperventilate, I looked at my phone. Damn. No new messages from twenty-three seconds ago. And there he was, two feet away from me.

"Everything okay?" he asked with a smile, tilting his head and raising his eyebrows. And once again my mind left the premises, and I stared blankly at his sensual mouth. And lips. Teeth. Smile.

Wait. He asked a question. Normal people responded to questions.

This impassiveness was not normal behavior for me. Being asked a question was normal. Answering it was normal. Being snarky was normal. Being stunned by a man, so not normal.

I rallied and said, in my most loquacious manner, "Yeah."

Then I rallied again and said the most banal thing to ever come out of my mouth: "The coffee is really good here." And then I cringed, and waited for the blowback from him when he realized that I had nothing intelligent to say.

Surprisingly, he looked even brighter. "I source it from small, family farmers in Kona, and roast the beans here. You gotta have a passion, you know?"

Passion. What did he mean by passion? I didn't have passion in my life.

But maybe passion was what I really needed?

"Passion," I said out loud without meaning to.

Now he was a foot away from me and I could smell him. Damn, he smelled good. Clean, but musky. Mansmell. Now that's a word too, I thought. Manflesh and mansmell.

He lowered his voice and said the sexiest thing ever: "I'm all about passion. And coffee is not my only one."

So if there had been any question before, he had me. I wanted to know about all of his passions and I wanted to know, like, yesterday.

Then I thought about what else he said. Was he the manager? Why was he wiping down tables if his job is to source coffee?

"You source coffee?"

"Yeah." So he was loquacious too? Good to know. He didn't elaborate, but raised an eyebrow in invitation. "Come back. I'll show you more."

All I could think about was what "more" of him I wanted him to show me. It was mostly located under his black, Southwinds coffee shop apron, although the exposed body parts looked damn fine, too.

The snob part of me—sorry, but there was one—wanted to know what I was doing flirting with a coffee shop manager. Slumming it. Yeah, I could be a real bitch. Sorry, not sorry.

The part of me that was throbbing between my legs did not care.

I nodded. "I'll come back. I have to get to court right now but I have a trial next week and will be down this way." Damn, girl. I said more than three words at a time to him. High five!

"Then I expect to see you here every day next week at Southwinds, Movie Star." Movie Star? Oh, then I blushed. And other places on my body suddenly became wet. How could he do this? Perhaps since he radiated heat, parts of me were melting.

It was dawning on me that after depression it was so nice to feel something, *anything*, but it was especially nice feeling these erotic sensations caused by this hunky man in a coffee shop.

I forced myself to look back at him and he looked at me curiously, like he really wanted to know whether I would come back to the coffee shop. I had to be back here all next week for trial, but truthfully, and lawyers are in the truth business, I'd figure out an excuse to come back anyway. It was going to be hard to keep my mind on my work instead of thinking about the solar system all week. But I could do it. Maybe.

"Okay," I whispered.

Court went as well as it could, and I left the courthouse, starting the final countdown until the trial the following week. Because it was lunchtime, I decided to grab a burrito from Johnny's for a late lunch, and brought it to the parking lot by the beach in Ventura. I pulled my convertible up to the surf-side pay lot and parked between a cool, old Ford pickup truck and a restored VW bus. Although it was normally windy in the afternoons, it was comfortably breezy. I put down the top of my car, and unwrapped my yummy goodness of simmered beef and cheese in a hot tortilla. A habit. These days it seemed that the only pleasures I got were from food.

I took a bite and watched the bicyclists, walkers, joggers, runners, and roller bladers go by on the paved path that wended its way between the parking lot and the beach. Picnickers lingered nearby on a grassy bluff beyond the walkway, before the rocks and sand, playing loud reggae music. Six seagulls plotted an attack on the picnickers' cheese puffs, by slowly surrounding them and hopping forward furtively. The slight wind through the evenly placed palm trees made them sway. I had a good view of the surfers. The waves came into shore, small and regular, and there were plenty of surfers out on the waves. The sun sat overhead, although not directly, and it made the water sparkle. Just the place to relax.

I knew that I needed to get back to the office and stay late doing trial prep, but sustenance was important, too. I was careful not to unwrap too much of my burrito at once, and was rewarded for my efforts by not getting any of it on me or my suit. I sipped my Diet Coke, abiding by the ancient girl law that required you to order a diet drink when you indulged in way too many calories from food. As I not-so-daintily inhaled my burrito, I watched as a group of surfers made their way out of the water.

The black, wetsuited bodies waded in the shallow tide, surfboards under their arms. They walked along the sand below the parking area, heading towards the rocks between the sand and the grassy picnic area.

I realized, as I watched a small group of four of them, that the body of one of them looked familiar.

Very familiar.

I held my breath. I realized that it was him. Of course, it was him. Sun God. Damn gravitational pull. I'd recognize those sunny, curly, shiny, dark blond locks anywhere.

Ryan walked out of the water, a Channel Islands short board under his arm, made his way carefully across the sand by the water, and gingerly up the rocks to the parking lot, which was up on a small bluff. He stopped at the patch of grass directly in front of my car, about twenty yards away. He hadn't noticed me, but I had a good view of him from my vantage point. He set his surfboard down carefully, and used the long cord on his back to slowly, oh so slowly, pull the zipper down on the back of his wetsuit, first taking out one arm, then the other, so that the wetsuit folded down. He was bare-chested.

Now there was a sight.

Golden skin. Broad shoulders. Narrow waist and hips. Surprisingly, no tattoos. He was lanky and lean, but defined. Wet looked good on him.

He grabbed a towel that had been left on the grassy area and ran it through his hair so that it was going every which way—making him even more sexy, if that was possible—and then he dried off his torso. *Don't mind me*, I thought as I stared. I was just perving on a coffee shop surfer dude. Nothing to see here.

His buddies joined him soon after, and he talked with them quietly, though I couldn't hear what he was saying with the sound of the waves and the seagulls and the reggae stoner music from the picnickers. At one point, he stretched his arms overhead and some more muscles popped. Yeah, that was nice scenery. Nope, not looking at his back. Nor his ass. Nope. Not me.

After a bit, he picked up his surfboard, his towel wrapped around his neck, and turned away from the beach and toward me.

I got a shot of abs. Wow. His wetsuit hung down his hips and displayed the most beautiful surfer abs. They were taut, lean, and ended in a V, which went to, ahem.

Then he saw me and walked straight toward me. As he came closer, it was all I could do not to drool over the leather interior of my car. Holy happy trail. Right down below his belly button. Where his wetsuit was hanging. Yep. There. Did I mention happy trail?

I was definitely losing it.

"Amelia."

He remembered my name. That was a good thing because around him, I plainly forgot it. I also forgot my snark. And everything else. He smiled at me and then walked past, turned, and set the surfboard and towel in the bed of the truck next to me.

Seriously?

I'd parked next to the Sun God.

What were the odds?

After he set it down, he came back to me and leaned up against the driver's side of my car, where my arm rested on the door, since the windows and convertible top were still rolled down. His six-pack abs touched my knuckles and I flinched. His body felt cold from the ocean, covered in goose bumps. But *oh my*, he was a sexy man. He looked like an ad for Quicksilver or O'Neill or something, with his wetsuit folded down. Heck, he probably modeled for them for all I knew. I really wanted to get to know those abs.

Instead, I breathed out a "Hey." He looked down at me, his freckles popping in the sunlight, and grinned, with the towel still around his neck.

"Did you kill them in court?" Court? Court? What court?

Oh yeah.

I finally—finally!—remembered my swagger. Glory and hallelujah. "Yeah, pretty much. I killed it." I managed a grin. He looked at me with a question in his eyes.

"Good. As I suspected. Do you surf?"

"Nope. Just watch surfers." Okay, so now I was blatantly flirting. His grin grew, if that was even possible.

"Any in particular?"

I nodded, straight-faced, pretending to be very serious. "Only one, really."

God, I wanted to jump his bones. I think I was drooling, or at least licking my lips, at the abs that were not eighteen inches from my tongue. Even though I felt embarrassed by my boldness in flirting, I could not help myself. It was thrilling to feel emotions. I'd never been more attracted to a person in my life. And apparently the feeling was mutual, given his boner in the coffee shop.

He looked at me thoughtfully, then his eyes blazed with intensity.

"Now you know another passion of mine," he said in his low voice. "So what's your passion?"

All I could think about was that it was probably residing in his pants. Before I could help myself, I blurted, "I don't know, but I'd like you to help me find out."

Horrified, I realized that I had taken the flirting too far—at least for me—and I needed to escape. I'd never been this obvious to a man, ever, in my life.

At the same time, it was kind of fun and liberating.

I pressed the ignition and shifted the car into reverse, and made to drive away, my foot still on the brake, my only instinct to flee. As I did, Ryan leaned over the door before I could get away, and said, "I will." Then he leaned in and kissed me hard, straight on the mouth.

I was shocked. Like, literally, he shocked me with his lips and I felt static electricity pulsing from my mouth, then down my neck and into my belly. His lips were cold from the ocean and he smelled like salt and the sea, but oh, so good, then I groaned and opened my mouth, and he slid his tongue in next to mine. Now that was hot. I couldn't help myself, but with my foot on the brake, the car parked, my engine roaring, I started exploring the inside of his mouth with my tongue, and it was very warm and inviting there.

My brain then, finally, caught up with my body and realized that I was kissing Ryan from the coffee shop. He was kissing me. We were kissing. Yum.

I couldn't process.

I also didn't want to stop.

After an eon or so—or maybe it was a nanosecond, I couldn't tell time these days since I didn't wear a watch anymore—he closed his mouth, gave me a last closed mouth kiss and stood up, arms straight on the car door. I pulled back, stunned, and looked at him, my lips sensitive and full. Yeah, that was the best kiss I had ever received. Hands down. No question. Best kiss ever.

And I may have had burrito breath, but he didn't seem to care.

"You're beautiful," I blurted. Then my cheeks reddened, and I flushed like it was the hottest day of the year. It was also hard to ignore the throbbing throughout my body that settled in my nether region. He stepped back and looked at me softly, an eyebrow cocked up.

I decided that this was way too much to process right now. Too much. After being numb for so long, feeling flooded with sensation was overwhelming, and I needed to get away to process.

Although a part of me thought that grabbing him seemed like a good idea, instead, I let my foot off the brake and on to the gas, backing up. Thank all that's holy that I didn't run over his foot.

Once I put the car in drive and the coast was clear, I floored it. As I pulled out of the parking lot, I could see him in my rear view mirror, still looking at me as I drove away.

I was not sure why I left so fast. Just that it was so strange to feel … anything. And to want to feel more. I thought this was a good thing. So, why did I feel the need to escape even when I knew I'd be back for more? And why was I so struck by him?

I didn't believe in this fairy tale romance nonsense. I was an educated, enlightened woman, and I did not need a man. I had a job, a house, a car, and a life. I did not need *anyone*.

So why did he affect me so much?

FOUR

Good Catholic Girl

FOLLOWING MY COURT APPEARANCE and kiss with Ryan, I drove along the beach back to work. The life of a lawyer sucked sometimes. Actually, it sucked most of the time. No wonder I had been clueless when Ryan asked me about passion. I wouldn't know what passion was if it sent me a text. Nevertheless, once I got to the office, I focused, and I managed to get more trial preparation done; I felt confident that we would be ready for the following week.

After wolfing down some pretzels in the breakroom at work for dinner, I finally stumbled into my house at eleven o'clock that night. My house welcomed me, as it always did. I lived in a tiny, adorable adobe with two bedrooms and one mint green vintage bath. Even though it was small, it had cost a fortune because of where it was located: in the tony hills of S.B. Like most of the area, my house had classic white stucco exterior walls, window trim painted turquoise green, and a red tile roof. It also had a small, but cute yard, which the gardener certainly kept in order. But I was never around to enjoy it.

Inside, I had decorated my comfortable living room with dark brown leather couches, and cushy twill armchairs—that I never sat in because I worked all day. My galley kitchen boasted small high-end appliances—that I never used because I lived in my office, and ate out all the time. At night, I slept in a luxurious bed—that I had shared for only part of one night, for the last year and then some.

Yeah.

No wonder I was depressed.

When I walked in, though, it felt good to be home. All day, I had ignored the throbbing between my legs, which had been steadily increasing. Even though I was working, I kept having daydreams about Ryan and his kiss. And his abs. And his tented pants. All. Day. Long.

Dammit.

I felt so sexually frustrated. Okay, I'd been sexually frustrated for a very long time. At least I admitted it now. Today, Ryan certainly brought it to a head. But I didn't know what to do.

Frankly, I was tempted to take care of it myself. I never did. That was against the Rules.

Okay, so about my Rules. I hadn't told my therapist about them yet and I realize that they were, well, prudish. They were arbitrary, too. I didn't care. I came up with my Rules to keep my feminism and my dignity and my badassery and I was not about to change them. I had sex. On my terms.

At least that was what I had told myself when I came up with my Rules.

Okay, so I came up with my Rules in high school when I still thought that French kissing was gross. After reading a million teenage magazines, guide books, and warnings about abstinence, rape, pregnancy, diseases, and heartbreak, I'd believed that making clear boundaries about what I would and would not do with my body would establish, firmly, that I was in charge. At that time, admittedly, it was probably a good idea. A teenage girl needs to take it slowly—the scary dangers discussed in the magazine articles were real. Every woman needed to learn how to own her own body and deal with the emotions that sex introduced into her life. I wasn't sure, however, whether I had developed sexually since high school. Truthfully? Probably not.

Further, at the time that I established them, I had no role models and no one to talk to about my Rules. No one had ever talked to me about sex. I mean, yeah, I had sex education in school, but I didn't have anyone to talk to about it for real. Not my mom. Not my dad. I was an only child. And while I gossiped about sex with my friends, none of us really had any idea what we were talking about, since none of us had done it. I had no feminine mentor to guide me through sexual development. And after I developed my list, the Rules became ingrained in me and I kept them throughout everything that happened to me.

Of course I had some very strong hormones that led me to lose my virginity when I became legal. Um, yeah, lawyer. I had no rule against premarital sex; it just had to be missionary. None of the guys in college seemed to mind.

Or him. But I didn't want to think about him.

So there. Yes, I had sex. But I'd never been too creative with it, or allowed any guy to be too creative with me. Like at all creative. Like not even oral sex creative. Which I admit was not really pushing the bounds of sexual creativity at all.

Okay, it's totally fucked up.

But the thing was, I knew now that I'd outgrown the reasons for the Rules, and I'd just been too stubborn to change them. I was fully aware that at my age, there was no logical reason for them. And I knew, if I thought about it, that there was more going on with my Rules than I admitted to myself: fear; guilt; a need to keep myself safe and protected; a need not to be vulnerable with anyone; a need to not trust anyone. I had talked about these things with my therapist, weekly, in other contexts. If I didn't let anyone in, sexually or otherwise, then I couldn't get hurt.

The thing was, this wasn't true. I had been hurt, and hurt badly, even with my Rules.

Maybe I really didn't know anything at all about it, even though I thought I did. It was likely that I didn't even know what good sex was.

But today, this feeling between my legs and in my brain—I couldn't ignore it.

Sure, previously, I'd tried masturbating and it never got me anywhere. The combination of the guilt—even if I didn't acknowledge it—and the belief that I couldn't show any interest in anything sexual made me not even go there.

Right now, though, I was suffering. I was really suffering and I needed a release. More than I ever had. Those damn antidepressants just couldn't rule me like this. It had been a year since I'd come. At least. I could do this. I had to get me some, somehow, some way. Even if I gave it to myself.

A decision made, then.

I just stood there, in my house, staring without seeing, and then, as if an invisible force was propelling me forward, I headed straight for my bedroom and crashed into my bed, all in. If I could have sex with men, with or without guilt, I could have sex with myself, and guilt had nothing to do with it. I'd invented my own new brand of feminism.

Fuck the guilt. Fuck the denial of pleasure. Fuck the idea that I couldn't be openly sexual. Fuck it all. I didn't know about crossing all of the Rules off of my list, but I sure as hell was going to cross one off. Tonight.

Not bothering to take off my clothes or high heels, I stroked my hands inside my clothes, along my skin, down my body, noting my fleshy curves. Yep. All me.

Those breasts? All me. That little pouch on my belly? All me.

I noticed that my skin was very soft.

I'd never noticed how soft before.

I kept going, uncertainly touching my pubic hair. Idly, I wondered if I should remove it and be bare. That wasn't something I'd ever considered, but now it seemed to be in the way.

Wait. Focus. Masturbation. Yeah, what a word. Almost as good as manflesh. Or mansmell.

Focus, Amelia.

My last thought was, oh hell, I'm going in.

With a tentative graze, I touched myself, realizing that I was all wet, and had been all wet all day. My panties were soaked. For Ryan.

But also just for me.

My sexuality mattered.

I pressed into the flesh at the front of my pubic bone instinctively, because it felt good there. I could feel a vein throbbing. I stopped stroking, and let go for a moment, and then realized that it would feel better if I kept going than if I stopped. Huh. Maybe this was where my cute, little orgasm had been hiding. Not with my antidepressants or with Paul the accountant, but with me, with my desire.

I'd never felt such desire before. Of course there were hormones coursing through my body when I lost my virginity. And I certainly felt something for him. Ugh, him. But when my depression entered, my desire left, and my orgasm was nowhere to be seen.

Now, I desired Ryan. The Sun God of my dreams. Mr. Passion.

I reached down further and explored. I could just see his eyes and freckles. His golden skin. Those abs. The V.

The V did it. Sexy fucking body. That kiss. Cool skin and hot mouth. I started to pant. Oh my God, I made myself pant.

I felt like I deserved a trophy for panting.

Setting aside an errant thought of my repressed past—why oh why did I think of things at times like this?—I stroked and caressed, pressing my folds, moving my fingers wherever it felt good.

After a bit, I added the fingers from my other hand. One hand had a finger inside while the other parted my skin and rubbed my clit, faster and faster.

Because I was so sensitive and desperate from being distracted by thoughts of Ryan all day, I got a little wetter, I could smell myself, my muscles got a little tighter, my world closed in so that it was nothing but my own pleasure, and lo and behold, the dawn of an orgasm arrived. I could tell: my body started to tense, I clenched my muscles, it felt oh-so-good, and I stroked and I stroked, and then, finally, finally, the shuddering, the release, which I had not felt for so long, and my brain was bathed in pleasure, my body quivering and happy.

Ta-da!

Now I really wanted a trophy. The orgasm was good, although not earth shattering, but I was almost in tears because my body still worked.

I was alive!

The Prozac hadn't stolen my orgasm.

Or if it had, I'd stolen it back.

Still, funnily enough, it surprised me and took me over so quickly that I stopped stroking, and then realized, again, with some embarrassment, to myself that only I would notice, that I had to keep going. So I did. I felt my sex convulse and contract. That felt very good. Frankly, it also felt naughty. I could get over that.

Maybe.

Okay, so I looked around as if someone was going to catch me. I'd finally broken a Rule.

But wow. I should've done this a long time ago. I could almost feel the power of the release in my brain. The good hormones, or whatever the fuck it was that got released when you had an orgasm, were bathing my brain with the good shit, and I felt relaxed. Sated. Whole. Hmmm. The fucking antidepressants didn't own me.

I wondered how many other Rules I should break?

So I knew that it was late and that I should go to sleep, but I needed to figure out where I knew Ryan from. He clearly seemed to know me. Had I met him at Harvard? If so, what was he doing managing a coffee shop? I didn't mean to be a snob, but still.

Yeah, I was a snob. Deal with it.

Maybe he was a friend of my parents? No. A friend of a friend? No. I have friends, but not that many. And I would remember him. So did I know him from childhood? I had no idea. I grew up around here. Maybe he went to Waterford High?

After I cleaned up and put on my pajamas, I went to my bookshelf and pulled out my high school yearbooks. I started with my freshman yearbook and went through the names, looking for all the Ryans. I found a few but they weren't him. I looked in the sections for sophomores, juniors, and seniors. While there were some Ryans, I didn't see him.

Maybe he was younger than me. It could be hard to tell. I pulled out another book. And another. Finally, I got to my senior year.

Now I was completely distracted. It was way past midnight, after I had been working crazy hours, and I was reading things that people had written to me more than a decade before. My back was tired from sitting on the floor, surrounded by yearbooks, and I was remembering people and pictures and events from a long time ago. There were a lot of memories in those yearbooks. Yeah, I was the bomb in high school.

I wondered what I was now.

Finally, I paged to the freshman section of my senior year and there he was: *Ryan Kyle Fielding*. He looked little and sweet, with big eyes, a tan, and surfer hair, even at that age. He was adorable. But I didn't remember him. I wondered why he remembered me. On that thought, I crawled into bed, hoping to sleep some before I had to get up early, and start being a lawyer again.

The institutional fluorescent lights overhead sped by as I was pushed down

the bright, white hospital corridor, strapped to the gurney.

One light. Two lights. Three lights.

I stopped counting as I looked up at the nurses' faces as they rushed me to the operating room. Two women and a man, moving me down the hall. There was a rail along the walls, for protection.

I couldn't even walk.

They wheeled me into the operating room with an enormous light—high powered wattage, illuminating everything.

I'd never seen a light so big.

I was prepped for surgery. They gave me a shot in my arm. I didn't know what it was. They added something to my IV. I didn't know what that was either.

The anesthesiologist said that it was morphine and that I would soon start to feel it.

I did.

The anesthesiologist asked me if I could feel my belly.

What belly?

No, I couldn't.

Then it all went black and I couldn't see any more lights.

And then I woke up in my room, sweating.

Another fucking nightmare.

FIVE

Homework

MY PHONE VIBRATED with a text.
Staying sane?

My buddy Hugo had sent it. I met him at the mental hospital when I'd checked myself in. I *loved* the fact that I had a close friend from a mental hospital. It led to interesting answers to the question, "Where did you two meet?" We were the same age, and we clicked in therapy sessions, and while going through the program.

I found recovery from my suicidal ideations to be easier with a friend. We understood each other's issues and we understood that sometimes we just needed to talk with someone. So our friendship worked on a lot of levels. He was one of the few who knew all of my secrets.

A beautiful man, half Caucasian, half African-American, he had greenish eyes, dark skin, tattoos, and serious biceps. Time at the gym meant that he had a brawny body, which matched his rough-around-the-edges personality. He was also bisexual and extremely sexual, at all times, with essentially anyone attractive and available.

And he was a felon, which frankly made me laugh, because even though I was a lawyer, I was also prissy; I didn't hang out with criminals, except him. His felony conviction stemmed from some marijuana charges that he got before he received his marijuana card. Well, that plus selling to an undercover police officer in San Diego. And some other, um, crimes. I liked to tease him about it. But we had a lot in common since he liked Harry Potter too. Well, specifically, he liked Lee Jordan's character, and told me about it in intricate, sexual detail. Perv.

Never was sane, darling.

Me neither. Busy?

Oh, and he repeatedly asked me out. Even though he lived with a woman, he checked Tinder—and Grindr—constantly, and he spent his time constantly trying to hook up with, well, humans, including me.

Yep. Trial. Will need to blow off some steam after though.

After I sent that text, I questioned it. I couldn't go drinking with him because he was an alcoholic and I wasn't. But of course he picked up on my text in a different way:

I can help you with that.

Flirt. Still, I was used to fending him off.

Love ya darling but never.

Never say never.

I texted my friend Marie, the one who has been by my side since third grade.

Hugo flirted with me again.

I felt a bit like I was tattling, but I normally told her everything. She knew how good-looking he was, but she also knew how flirty he was since he flirted with her, too.

That boy …

Then I realized that I hadn't told her about Ryan. That discussion would need to be done in person, I thought.

Yeah. Come play with me after trial is done? Need to drink.

Wouldn't miss it.

She certainly wouldn't, the party girl.

I spent the remainder of my week and the weekend preparing for trial. But finally, our exhibit books were made, trial briefs marked, pretrial motions all taken care of, and I'd spent more time than I cared to preparing my client and other witnesses for their testimony. In the back of my mind lurked my homework from my therapist.

Was I really buying a vibrator? Breaking my rule of no toys? Did that count as a toy? It wasn't, like, a spanking bench. Maybe I would just buy a book. So much for focusing on my trial.

I became an attorney six years ago, and after the next year I'd be considered for partnership. The mid-size firm that I worked for in Santa Barbara had a great clientele, region-wide presence, and dedication to excellence. Or so we told ourselves and our clients. But seriously, it was a great place. Since I was "just" an associate attorney, and had not been promoted to partner—meaning that I was an employee, not an owner of the company—I worked with a partner on this trial as his second in command. The first-in-command partner was gorgeous, intense, and clearly not interested in me: Jake Slausen.

Four years older than me, and practically a foot taller, Jake embodied the definition of tall, dark, and handsome. During these late nights, I totally ogled his blue eyes—I swore they were made out of cut gemstones—and chiseled cheekbones. I just hoped that I did it in stealth-mode. He was good looking in a way that was completely distracting. Lucky for me, he was also completely unavailable because one, I worked for him and two, he was a serious workaholic. A further good thing, for me, was that his personality stunk. He had no time for anything but work. I had heard from the guys in the office that if they needed to talk to him, they had to follow him down the hall and talk in the bathroom because he wouldn't take the time to talk in his office if he was focused on a case. Weirdo.

Nevertheless, eye candy was always a good thing.

By Sunday night, we were as ready for the trial as we were going to be and I went home. I decided that what my bank thought of me didn't matter—it probably didn't scrutinize the purchases on my statements anyway—so I downloaded six naughty books on my e-reader and bought a deluxe vibrator from some Swedish company, paying for expedited shipping. I had a break on Monday because the trial didn't start until Tuesday. In the meanwhile, I had a few appointments to keep.

The next day I went to my therapist. Even though our trial would begin the following day, I made a point to see my therapist. I might even add an extra day this week because of the increased stress of trial—and the way a certain Sun God affected me.

"Have you been having any fantasies lately about suicide?"

"No, not anymore." I said. Then I admitted in a quiet voice, "Other type of fantasies, though."

She smiled.

I need to stop here and mention the name of my therapist: Christian Gray. With an "a" in Gray. And she's a woman. She was a lightly plump, elegant African-American, with bright eyes. Nevertheless, it made me giggle to no end to put a date with Christian Gray on my calendar each week. Not that I had read *That Book*. *That Book* was for other people, not me. I read Shakespeare. Well, that and the six books that I had downloaded on my e-reader. But I digress.

Something that I had learned from my therapy sessions over the past year was that a definition of depression was "anger turned inward." Perhaps. Before, I didn't even know that I was angry: Angry at my ex. Angry at God. Angry for what I had lost. Angry for the way my life was turning out. Angry at wasting my time feeling guilty or depressed about things that were part of my upbringing or environment, but were not who I really was. I was moving past all of those things. Now that I had processed some of the anger, it had opened me up to being able to feel other things. Therapy also helped me realize that the depression was not my fault, which was something easy to say, but not easy to believe. Nevertheless, as I talked with my therapist about the guilt that I felt about my sexuality, I knew that I had a lot more to do. Including a few more homework items before I went to trial the next day.

After I left my therapist and drove to my next appointment, I wondered if I'd ever see Ryan again. All I needed to do was go to the coffee shop and see him. I wondered if I could just take him behind the counter and have my way with him. He didn't seem like he'd mind.

It's funny. As a lawyer, advocating for my clients, I was used to being cocky, saying my mind, and arguing. But when it came to myself,

I could be shy and often I wouldn't ask for what I wanted. I needed to work up the nerve to see Ryan again—and then to be brave enough to actually talk with him and be myself with him. And then I wanted to see where it would go.

"YEEEE-OWWWWWWW!!!!!"

I could taste blood in my mouth.

That *HURT*. *Fuck!*

I sat, no, lay on my back in a small, white room at a salon. I wore nothing under my belly button, and the bottoms of my feet pressed together so that I looked like a frog. Yeah, I felt exposed. And holy hell, that hurt like a mother.

Thankfully, the friendly, but no-nonsense, attendant made this completely surreal situation bearable. She merrily told me that she had done this to all of her friends. So she didn't have issues about ripping the hair off of a hoo-ha or anywhere else down there. I didn't even know you could get hair in some of those places. I guess I'd never explored those parts.

Now that I thought about it, it was pretty funny that I had yelled so loud. I was normally a quiet, retiring sort of girl.

Well, sometimes.

But after a few more applications of warm wax, a few more rips, and a dash of a spray, she deemed me fit for consumption—so to speak.

I hastily put on my panties and pants and shoes and felt very, very funny in that sensitive area. It was now an ultra-sensitive area.

Smooth, waxed, and ready. Now I needed to walk out of here and face the receptionist and pay. Funny how that embarrassed me. Like, uh-oh, she knows what I did.

I found myself signing up for a year's worth of waxing.

As I made my way to my car, I passed a lingerie shop that I noticed on the way in.

What the hell, I thought. *Might as well do that too.*

I normally wore matching bras and panties, but nothing special. I usually shopped for underwear in nude, white, or black, and it certainly was nothing that I wanted to be photographed in for a boudoir shot.

But when I walked in the store, the beautiful red satin, black lace over cream, and turquoise lingerie struck me as something necessary to living.

The saleslady, who must have been about seventy years old, and looked tough as nails, said, "Need some help?" She scared me a little bit. Still. Onward.

"Uh, yeah." I was loquacious with her too.

"Have you been measured lately?" she asked briskly.

"Uh, no."

"Let's get you in here."

She pushed me into an elegant, but tiny room to change in, and climbed in there with me, seriously invading my personal space. Before I knew it, she poked, prodded, and announced my bra size. "Honey, I've been doing this so long I don't need a measuring tape. I'll be back, wait here."

I waited for just a moment, and she returned, loaded down with gorgeous bras, and gave me one to try on.

She stepped out, I put it on, and opened the curtain tentatively to show her. She came in and invaded my personal space again, by adjusting straps and the cups (hello, girls), and then she stepped back to admire her handiwork.

"That's lovely, dear."

I looked in the mirror. She was right.

A lavender bra, with underwire and lace, held me up in all the right places, and my girls were in there like little eggs in a nest. Or something. But it made me look … right. I looked sexy.

I wanted more.

"I'll take it," I said, and she gave me a pleased smile. "And the matching panties."

An hour later, I loaded up the trunk of my car with bags of pretty lingerie wrapped in tissue paper. I'd never owned so many pretty, lacy things. I treated myself to nice things sometimes, and dressed professionally, but I normally didn't go for the overtly sexy look. But these purchases were a treat just for me and were something that only I would know about.

And perhaps a certain surfer.

SIX

Trial

EARLY TUESDAY MORNING, I drove my car back to Ventura, along the coast again. This time Jake, my coworker and boss, took over the passenger seat. I was amazed that he'd asked me to drive since the fact that he was older than me, a partner, my boss, and male, would normally mean that he would pull rank and drive. Apparently he wanted to do research on his tablet, while we were driving the half hour or so to the courthouse. Something as simple as driving had me thinking about feminism. Guess it was just part of me.

We'd stuffed the trunk of my car with boxes of files, papers, and binders. Major butterflies hit above their weight class in my stomach, and I tried to ignore them. I also tried to clear my brain of all of the work-related anxiety I felt, as I drove and looked at the ocean and watched for pelicans.

We were headed to trial, finally.

Jake's tall, muscular body dominated my car's leather interior. I glanced at him and noticed that he was all spread out, long legs and body everywhere. Guys sometimes sat like they were invading conquerors.

Even though I didn't have a crush on Jake, I'd say it: it was hard to be with him in close proximity and remain professional, because he was such a hot distraction. He smelled *like a man* and was wearing a pristine suit and tie, his blue eyes glinting, his hair tousled but sober. Such a sexy physicality. I told myself that there was nothing wrong with ogling. I was just appreciating the art, people.

Okay, so maybe I was lying about the whole "I didn't have a crush on Jake" thing. Still, he was no Sun God.

With an energy completely unwelcome this early in the morning, he chattered the whole way about the trial, like a sexy, deep-voiced chipmunk. He lived for courtroom work. He wanted to be a statesman-like, Atticus Finch-type lawyer—at least before the second book was published and Atticus was reviled instead of revered. But I digress.

I wondered if he could talk about anything else. Well, it wasn't like I needed to see him at home over a dinner table, so it didn't really matter.

I struggled to listen to him, since I was still early-morning sleep-deprived. I needed coffee or else I was going to contemplate inflicting serious bodily harm on Jake Slausen, gift to women's eyeballs everywhere. He was probably a gift to gay men, too. To stop myself from plotting his destruction, I interrupted his discussion of the finer points of his opening statement.

"Jake, can we stop for coffee before we get there?"

"Sure, Amelia."

Of course a trip to get coffee would lead to an orbit around the Sun God—or at least a chance of being sucked into his tractor beam. I was ready for him.

Maybe.

Today I wore full lawyer badass gear, not fucking around this time. I donned the blue pinstripes and put my hair up in a chignon. But while I was physically put together, I still needed to get my brain awake for trial. Must insert caffeine. I pulled into the parking lot at Southwinds and Jake unfolded his long body from my Mercedes and entered with me, holding the door for me, like a gentleman.

Again, it was busy in the coffee shop. Again, it smelled divine. Again, there was a long line. And again, Ryan was there. This time I saw him immediately as I got in line, listening to Jake, who was standing very close to me, talking in my ear, so that I could hear him over the din. I grabbed a yogurt. Jake did too.

Ryan lit up when he saw me, but his eyes narrowed when he saw Jake standing so close, leaning into me as he spoke. When I got up to the counter, I learned that Ryan's effect on me was unchanged, although I was hopeful that this time I would be able to formulate words and speak them aloud, resulting in an order of a latte without major embarrassment. It appeared that my effect on Ryan was unchanged also, judging by the way he leaned up against the counter. This could be interesting.

"Hey, Movie Star," he greeted me.

I responded, "Hey," and ordered a latte with wild success. (I said, "I'd like a latte please." It was going well.) Jake ordered one too, and put his yogurt next to mine, handing Ryan his credit card.

"Trial today?" Ryan asked. I nodded and went to answer, but Jake interrupted.

"I didn't know you were a regular, Amelia."

I shrugged.

Jake looked at me with interest and then turned to Ryan. "Amelia and I start trial in an hour."

"Good luck," said Ryan politely and then he handed me the duplicate receipt, even though Jake paid. "We're having a survey. If you could just fill this out, I'd appreciate it," he said, looking at me straight in the eyes, ignoring Jake, who had moved to the side, and the mob of people all around.

The paper said "PHONE NUMBER?"

I took it and followed Jake to the side. It wasn't even a debate whether I gave Ryan my phone number. I'd never been more affected by another person in my life. I was usually so closed off. Normally it took me a long time to warm up to people. I pretty much had only Marie to tell my secrets to, Hugo, to flirt with—or not—and the people at work to gossip with. Ryan got through to me immediately. If I gave him my phone number, this meant that he would have access to me on his terms, not mine.

I thought about it for a second more.

That was fine with me. I wanted to see where this would go. I found a pen in my purse, wrote down my number and grabbed my latte from the barista. On my way out the door, following Jake, I handed the receipt to Ryan, saying "here is my survey answer."

He took it, opened it, and smiled. Then he took care of the next customer.

At lunch I checked my phone. There was a text from an unknown number.

Slay them. — Ryan

I texted back: **I will**, echoing his words when he kissed me. I remembered my snark while texting. Good.

That evening, I dropped Jake back at the office, where I had picked him up that morning, and headed home, exhausted. I was so done. We had a good first day of trial. So good, in fact, that we were feeling confident, which was dangerous. Still, we'd properly prepared and needed to rest up for the next day. Having a trial was like studying for finals. It really wasn't a good idea to cram. You had to know what you were doing well ahead of time, and you had to get a good night's sleep so that you'd be mentally agile. I pulled up to my house, parked, and saw a package sitting on my front porch, leaning against the front door.

Oh yeah, next day air.

The night just got a little more interesting.

The Swedish website said that it was waterproof. Right now, a bath, followed by a naughty book and a vibrator to ease the ache caused by Ryan, sounded like a good thing. I grabbed the package, opened my front door, sorted through the mail, and sat on my couch to open up my present to myself. Discreet brown box packaging led to an elegant upscale black box. I opened it up. It looked like a wand.

Naughty Harry Potter thoughts immediately came to mind.

I got my phone out and took a picture, texting it to Marie with the caption, **Ollivander got me a special wand.** Then I immediately deleted the picture in case my mom saw my phone.

No, my mom didn't check my phone. I just felt guilty, still, you know? I mean, she could check my phone, right? Never mind the fact that I was thirty-one.

While I waited to hear from her, I went to the bathtub and started to fill it up with warm, scented water. My phone vibrated with her response:

I solemnly swear that I am up to no good.

I laughed and went to text her back and looked at my phone and then I felt like I was going to faint. I hadn't sent that photo to Marie.

The text was from Ryan.

Fuckity fuck shit damn fuckballs.

My stomach dropped.

Oh, fuck, I'd just texted him a picture of my new vibrator. This was definitely on the minus side. On the plus side, he appeared to know his Harry Potter.

I didn't know how to handle this. Luckily, he did it for me.

Dinner. Friday. Your place.

Sheesh, he was bossy.

Then I realized that he had asked me out on a date. Or a stay at home date. Whatever. I was going to see him again. But not before I messed with him a little bit, to get him back for seeing my new vibrator.

Are you asking me or telling me? If you're asking, you need to say "please"

He immediately responded:

Gorgeous Movie Star, I would really like to get to know you better. Are you available this Friday for me to bring you dinner?

Seriously? I melted.

Yes.

Mischief managed.

Oh, fuck, what was I getting myself into?

The second day of trial, Jake and I drove separately so that he could do something after the trial. Unfortunately, I'd also left very late, so I had no time to see Ryan that morning, despite being in the neighborhood.

I raced to court, parked, ran through security, and hoofed it up to our courtroom. When I arrived at our department, Jake stood there in the hallway with a strange look on his face.

"We settled."

I was completely taken aback and it took me a moment to process his words.

"What? What do you mean, we settled?"

"The other side caved. We're going to put it on the record, and then we're done," he said, with a combination of relief and disappointment.

This was another part of being a lawyer. The stuff you go to law school to do—to be in court and to go to trial—rarely happened because it was just too expensive and risky. In settling a case and not going to trial, a lawyer felt a disappointment somewhat like a surgeon consulting with a healthy patient who did not need surgery. In other words, the client was not displeased to avoid court. Just the lawyer.

A half hour later, we were done with finalizing the settlement in court before the judge, and Jake gave me the rest of the day off. I knew just where to go. I texted Marie that I had the evening free, and we arranged to go drinking that night. Then, I headed to Southwinds for some excellent coffee and hopefully, some Ryan-viewing.

SEVEN

The Supply Closet

I ARRIVED AT SOUTHWINDS, SAW HIS gorgeousness behind the counter, and ordered my latte, successfully, "for here." He grinned and gave me a sexy chin lift. Once I got my oversized, porcelain, white cup and saucer, I sat at a cafe table, and went through my phone alerts, out of reach of his overwhelming physical charms.

After a while, I realized that I'd been sitting in Southwinds for a long time, and I should be getting home. I'd lost track of time and of Ryan. He wasn't at the cash register. I gathered my purse and wandered down to the bathroom, which was in the very back of the shop, carrying the coffee shop key, attached, with zero dignity, to a large serving spoon. When I emerged, Ryan appeared in the hallway, walking towards me.

Before I could do anything, he suddenly walked into my space, grabbed the back of my head with one hand, my tail bone with the other, and pressed me up against the wall, his mouth one inch from mine. My breasts crashed against his hard, broad chest, and I got an up close and personal view of his "Ryan" nametag on his apron. Oh, and that sexy surfer face.

So of course this happened too fast for me to process.

In my daze, I noticed a combination of protectiveness and power from him. He shielded my head and ass from getting hurt, but he was still in control—and still slamming me up against the wall. I dropped the serving spoon with a clatter.

"You with him?" he asked, huskily. God he smelled clean and good.

I was amused that he was jealous of Jake. Jake was good looking, sure, but his boring, workaholic personality kept me from being attracted to him in any way other than as a distant observer. It was nothing like the seductive pull I felt towards Ryan. It was easy to answer him honestly.

"No. He's just a coworker," I responded in a quiet voice, an inch away from his mouth, looking into his eyes.

"Anyone else?" he asked, roughly.

"No," I whispered.

"Then you're with me." And he closed the gap between us instantly, his warm mouth kissing mine, all of his body pressed against mine.

I lost myself in his kiss, in his body, and dropped my purse to the ground, grabbing his tight ass, and pressing him into me with both hands. He hardened some and wow, it felt huge. He was a tall drink of water after all—it must be big. Our tongues fought for position, our hands wild all over each other's bodies, and he broke apart with a growl, staring at me.

"No control. I have no control with you."

"Me neither," I breathed.

This was apparently the right thing to say, because he grabbed my hand, bent down to pick up my purse and the key, hauled me into an adjacent storage room, and shut the door, locking it. The room had a small window with frosted glass, allowing in ambient light. He didn't turn on the fluorescent light overhead. Stocked with boxes of paper cups, lids, and paper towels, huge burlap bags of coffee, and industrial cleaning supplies, the air was infused with the heavenly scent of coffee.

In an instant, his mouth was back on mine, and it was the best place for it to be. I nipped at his lips, chased his tongue, and grabbed every part of him I could. I got to touch his hair.

I repeat, I got to touch his hair.

It felt unbelievably soft, with thick blond curls and golden glints. Without any control, I started untying his black Southwinds apron at his waist, and he ducked to take it off at the neck. I yanked his shirt out from his pants, wanting, needing to feel those abs that I had dreamt about.

Righteous.

His bare skin felt smooth, warm, and soft, and the muscles under his soft skin felt like nothing I had ever felt before—alive and vibrant with movement, but also tense and strong. I reached around and hugged his lower back, feeling the dimples from the muscles there, as he kissed my throat, sucking and licking his way down my neck. I moaned like I was faking it, but I wasn't.

His hands made the journey from my jaw to my back to my ass. Then, in an instant, he looked at me questioningly, and I understood immediately. After a week of new experiences with vibrators,

Brazilians, naughty books, a burrito kiss, and his boner behind the counter, no, I couldn't wait either. I gave him the go-ahead.

"Yes," I whispered, and he yanked up my skirt, pulled down my panties, and I stepped out of them. Then he slid one hand on my ass, the other hand between my legs, and then growled at what I was sure was nothing but wetness.

By the way, I have never had a man growl at me before, and I heartily recommend it. I nearly convulsed on the spot.

"You're bare. Holy fuck, that is sexy," he panted in my ear. "It's so soft. So wet. So sexy."

After days of thinking about him, I wanted him to take me wherever he wanted, even against the wall. I sucked on his ear and held on to him. His finger caressed my wet slit, circling my clit, entering me, and sliding out again. I knew that I was soaked and getting wetter by the touch.

"Christ," he said. "Your body is ready. Are you?"

"Yes," I said more strongly this time, looking at him directly in the eyes, and he didn't need any other encouragement. He continued to caress and stroke my clit, kissing my neck. He paused, then growled again, and took out his wallet from his back pocket, pulling out a condom.

I was busy wrestling with his belt, his buttons, and his zipper. After he ripped open the condom with his teeth, he threw the wallet on the floor by my purse, and helped me undo his pants. Between the two of us, we freed him, and in my daze and my panting, I caught a glimpse of the most impressive manhood that I had ever seen—long, thick, veiny, and hard.

Manhood. Another good word.

Focus, Amelia.

I didn't have to tell myself twice. He put on the condom in an instant, and backed me up to the wall.

"Wrap your legs around me," he ordered.

He was so strong, he lifted me up, then I wrapped my arms around his neck and my legs around his hips, and he pressed me against the wall. Then, holding my ass, he slipped his thick cock inside me, in one swift move. I'd never done this position before. I'd never had sex outside of a bed before. This was so hot. My body was so slick, it felt amazing.

I had never felt so full in my life.

I had never felt so good in my life.

I had never felt so whole in my life.

He looked me in the eyes, as he pressed himself to be fully seated within me, the tip of his cock all the way up and filling me entirely, and said, "You are the most beautiful woman there is, Amelia. You deserve to be worshiped, but right now I can't control myself. So hang on, okay?"

"Yes," I gasped.

He began to thrust, his cock coming out and in me, and it felt so good. No one had been this full into me. And I meant that in a lot of ways. Because I was holding on to him and braced against the wall, he brought a hand between us and started rubbing the exact right spot on my sex, all the while moving back and forth within me. I entered a state of bliss with this gorgeous guy, who was making me feel whole, making me feel pleasure, making me feel, period.

And then, after building up my sensitive tissues, he put me down and slid his cock out of me. I whimpered in protest, but he just kissed me again, spun me around, and said, "Brace against the wall."

Okay, now the rational part of me said, "I don't do this position." This was against my Rules.

But frankly, at this point, I didn't care. It was hot. I did as he said and he took a second to caress my butt cheeks, and then entered me from behind, his thick, long cock filling me even more than before.

Wow.

He sucked on my neck, and put one hand up my shirt, caressing my breasts through my bra. The other hand sought my clit and found it again.

I was in his complete control. He overwhelmed my senses, kissing me, stroking me, fondling me, and thrusting into me. Now that I was doing it, I wasn't sure why this position was on my no-no list. And the lawyer in me argued that strictly speaking, it wasn't doggy style. Perhaps it was on my list of prohibited sex rules because I couldn't see him, which made me vulnerable, and at the mercy of his whims. But boy could I feel him. And boy did I not want him to stop.

I decided to consider crossing "doggy style" off of my Rules.

In all of these activities, I didn't even think about my orgasm. I didn't worry about it, I didn't wonder where it was or whether it was going to come. I just felt good. I just felt.

But now that I thought about my orgasm, I could tell you something.

I was going to get one.

I could tell, he was going to make me come. The pleasure between my legs built and built, overwhelming me, drawing me to feeling more and more. "Oh my God, Ryan, this feels so good," I gasped, as the pleasure increased.

"You're going to come," he told me. And he was right. I could feel my body tightening. The combination of him filling me inside—all the way, all the empty parts were full—and pressing my outside was just too much, and I lost it.

There's a reason why they call the thing a climax. It's the highest or most intense point in the development of something. Well, that's what Google said. Ryan brought me to the highest and most intense point I had been in years. And he did it in a storage room in a coffee shop.

Amazing.

With a release I moaned, and again my brain was flooded with all of the good stuff. I couldn't think of anything but the intense pleasure wracking my body, exploding, making me feel wonder. My body buckled, and he moved his hands to hold my hips firmly, pulling them back towards him and supporting me fully. It was all I could do to keep my arms straight against the wall.

He increased the pace to an incredible speed, and I could tell that he was getting close, because his cock felt even thicker and fuller. He gasped a final sigh and said "Fuck, Amelia," and then collapsed into me, arms wrapped around me, holding me up and pressing me into the wall.

After a few moments, he pulled out, kissed my neck, pocketed the condom, and tucked himself back in, pulling his pants up, but not buttoning them yet. He grabbed my panties for me and straightened them, helping me to put one leg in and then another. Then he helped me straighten my skirt, and tucked in my blouse. He buckled his pants up and tucked in his shirt, looking at me intently.

I was overwhelmed. After more than a year of no orgasm and a sexual history of crap, this man could get me to orgasm in just a few minutes flat in this storage room. Um yeah, I'd like some more, please.

Even though he was bossy, he cared for me throughout. He cradled my head and my ass. He didn't forget about my purse. He helped me get dressed. I didn't know what the rules were for sex in a coffee shop storage room with the manager, but I knew that I liked it.

I managed a heartfelt, "Can we do that again?"

He laughed. "Abso-fucking-lutely. Text me your address, and I'll be there Friday night."

"I can do that," I responded, smiling shyly.

After he smoothed my hair and I messed with his, he gave me another kiss, this one sweeter, less desperate, but not less intense. "You look gorgeous. I'll come at seven and bring dinner. We'll go slowly. We'll explore. I guarantee that it'll be pleasurable."

"Okay," I agreed, and I reached up and kissed him again, his warm pouty lips on mine. After we stopped, he pulled back, smiled down at me, and then reached around and unlocked the supply room door.

Luckily no one was in the hall, so I didn't have to worry about how disheveled I looked. I hoped that no one had heard us.

He picked up the bathroom key attached to the serving spoon, deposited it on the counter, walked me all the way out of the store to my car, and then kissed me goodbye. I took off, noticing the sun along the water and singing along with the radio the whole way home.

EIGHT

Four Cosmos

I T ALL CAME CRASHING DOWN ON me that night, as I ordered my fourth cosmo with Marie.

I had felt a buzz, an energy, my entire drive back to Santa Barbara. I was happy, basking in the relaxation from my orgasm from Ryan, reveling in feeling something, anything, and excited about my date with him on Friday. The experience of getting up close and personal with the Sun God seriously rocked my world. Yummy yummy. Taking the rest of the day off of work cemented my good mood. It was like I had forgotten that I was ever depressed.

If you don't realize that's incredible, I'll tell you: that's incredible.

After going home, relaxing, and showering, I changed into dark jeans and a silky, dark purple camisole with a soft dark grey cashmere belted cardigan and stilettos. Then I took a taxi to meet Marie at the trendy watering hole on State Street that we frequented.

Already one sheet to the wind by the time I walked in, Marie greeted me with a squeal. She could be a bit loud. Worse when she was drunk. I loved her, anyway. She had saved my life, literally. I'd do anything for her. She was a tattooed, pierced, opinionated, vegan dynamo. Skinny, busty, foul-mouthed, with a limitless heart and hair that changed colors on a weekly basis. Today it was pink-ish, to match the cosmos. Beautiful and loud, she attracted plenty of attention from the group of frat boys sitting at the next table.

I proceeded to catch up to her, alcohol-wise, and grilled her about her recent activities. By the time I had downed cosmo number three and had ordered cosmo number four, I had told her everything about Ryan. Everything.

I thought that her shriek could be heard on the moon.

"YOU SLUT!" she screamed. The closest frat boys leaned in to listen.

My heart stopped. Ohmigod. She was right. I was a slut. I didn't know anything about him, and I had slept with him.

Wait. A misnomer. There was no sleeping involved.

No bed either, for that matter.

Correction: I had sex with him, standing up, and I'd barely spoken three sentences to him. Total slut.

Fuck.

Still.

Lawyer instincts kicked in, and I defended myself.

"I am the farthest thing away from a slut."

"I KNOW!" she yelled.

"And there's nothing wrong with being a slut."

"I KNOW!" she yelled.

"So why are you yelling?" I yelled back at her.

"I DON'T KNOW!" she yelled.

I was getting nowhere but drunker and drunker. The frat boys looked at each other, and at us, like they were going to speak, but instead they just grinned identically. Shit.

But then it dawned on me: I was banging the pool guy, so to speak. He just happened to be a surf bum/coffee shop manager, instead of the pool guy/gardener/plumber/repair guy/fireman, but I still belonged in bad eighties porn. Professional woman gets all her bedroom fantasies fulfilled by laborer. Now I know that's not a very nice thing to think. I've already admitted that I'm a snob. But this made me feel like I was using Ryan just to get over my depression. And if he was the pool guy, then I'm just using him.

Here's the good part about being a lawyer: I know how to argue.

Here's the bad part about being a lawyer: I know how to argue. Even with myself.

The "I'm a slut, I'm not a slut, it's not wrong to be a slut anyway" tug-of-war continued, for a while, in my brain, and then I resolved it, definitively. Well, definitively, for now. As definitive as I could be after four cosmos and while ordering a fifth.

"Marie, he's a gorgeous guy and I'm attracted to him. He's the sexiest thing I've ever seen. I want to see him again."

"Then do it," she said drunkenly, in a slightly lower decibel level than before.

I was so glad that we got that settled. The waitress delivered our drinks.

"I love you," I told her drunkenly and mushily.

"I love you too," she slurred back at me. The guys at the next table leaned closer to see what was going to happen next.

A few hours later, the bar called a taxi for me and I went to bed.

Hospital smells.

Bright lights.

A needle injecting me.

I can't feel anything.

The bright lights again.

I'm crying out.

I woke up in a sweat, frantic, looking around, but I was in my bed and there was no one else there.

The next day, I decided to call in sick, nurse my hangover, and meet with my therapist. While I waited for the time to leave for my appointment, I fired up my e-reader and started reading one of the erotic novels that Christian Gray had recommended for me. I realized something as I read the incredibly hot book: I'd never known that it was okay to get my panties wet. It happened to the heroine four times in the book. I'd never known that was normal. My mother used to tell me to bathe myself with a washcloth so I wouldn't ever touch myself. I thought that feeling turned on was a bad thing.

I was wrong.

I'd just been hearing my mom's voice in my head all these years. I could think for myself now. I was an adult. I loved getting nailed by Ryan in the supply closet at Southwinds. I wanted to find out where else we were going to do it. I couldn't wait until Friday night. I also realized something about the book. I had always assumed that erotica and porn were the same thing and I stayed away from both. Too naughty. But erotica was in black and white. Porn was in color. Erotica was words. Porn was pictures. Erotica appealed to women through their brains. Porn appealed to women through their eyes. Since I was the lawyer-type, it's obvious that the way to get me all hot and bothered was through my brain. I was slowly becoming a fan of erotica.

I want to kiss you on your lips and then explore where it will go.

Hugo, are you sure you meant to send this to me?

Oh yeah, baby.

I laughed out loud, reading his text while sitting in the waiting room for my therapist. Hugo'd never change. Then she called me in and I sat down.

"I've made some progress this week but I've also regressed." By smiling, Christian Gray encouraged me to continue. "I did your homework. I feel, uh, different. I bought the books, the lingerie, and the vibrator." We talked about how all of that felt. Then I blurted, "I, um, had sex with Ryan at the coffee shop."

She looked at me with an unreadable expression. "How did that make you feel?"

"Truthfully? Awesome. I'm not going to go be crazy promiscuous. But it was wonderful." She nodded. "I also slut-shamed myself." She nodded again.

"Are you going to see him again?"

"Tomorrow night."

"How does that make you feel?"

"I'm excited and I'm scared. I feel shame and fear that someone is going to get hurt or someone is not going to approve. And then I argue with myself that I don't have to feel that way."

Christian gently smiled. "Trusting and opening yourself up are healthy, but scary, feelings. When you've been depressed, it can take time to allow others in. Don't feel like you need to push yourself too hard at first. Do what comes naturally. But it's okay to feel whatever you feel. You may feel vulnerable. But trust that feeling."

On Friday, I went to work early before a court appearance and chatted with Neveah, our receptionist, before going into my office, checking my emails, and grabbing the client's file. As I headed away from her desk, Jake came in the building and followed me down the hall to my office, chatting about the settlement in our trial and the next matters that we were going to be working on. He seemed unusually relaxed, with his hands in the pockets of his lawyer trousers, and his blue eyes dancing.

"Any plans tonight, Amelia?"

"Yes, I do," I responded, startled.

"Too bad. I wanted to know if you wanted to go have a drink with me."

I was floored and then recovered. "Next time, perhaps."

"Sounds good." He turned on his heel and left for his office.

I sat in my chair, speechless.

WTF? First Hugo was stepping it up, now Jake? Was there something in the water? Did I give off extreme female pheromones now that I had an orgasm or two this week? I gathered the client's file and headed to court.

"All rise. The Superior Court of California, County of Santa Barbara is now in session, Honorable Hannah Morales, Judge

Presiding."

I hastily put my cell phone on silent as the bailiff called the court to order. The court was packed this morning with attorneys and litigants.

Then I waited for my case to get called.

And waited.

And waited.

While I waited, I saw a text from Ryan.

See you tonight. I'm bringing dinner.

I shivered. And other parts of me felt good.

Then I realized that the judge was looking at me and calling my case. I had not been paying attention. I snapped into lawyer mode and walked to the podium.

"Amelia Crowley, present, attorneys for the plaintiff."

LATER THAT AFTERNOON, I CALLED Marie from the Paseo Nuevo shopping center, in a panic, after I had texted her pictures of plates, placemats, table cloths, stemware, and candles. This was my way of dealing with the fact that I would be seeing Ryan in just a few short hours.

At my house.

"He's coming over, Marie. He's bringing dinner. I need new plates."

"Step away from the Pottery Barn, Amelia."

"But I give good table."

"Step away."

"But he's coming tonight!"

"Do I need to kick your ass? What you have is fine."

I sighed. She was right. I needed to head home and get ready for whatever Ryan had planned for tonight.

NINE

Appetizers and Dessert

A TALL, TAN, SURFER HUNK STOOD on my doorstep in the evening sun, his golden hair gleaming and his eyes sparkling.

Special delivery. For me.

He again wore a plaid, short-sleeved, button-down shirt, with a white t-shirt underneath, dark jeans, and flip flops. God, even his feet were attractive. The shirt hugged his biceps and the jeans hung, in a sexy way, down his hips. He carried two bouquets of small white rosebuds, and two Trader Joe's grocery bags.

"Hi!" I chirped, overly cheery. "Come on in." I wore a petal pink, cashmere, V-neck sweater and jeans. Comfy but elegant.

Oh, and I had on new lingerie underneath.

He looked down at me and smiled his Sun God smile. Then he stepped into my home, dropped the bags and the flowers on the foyer, and grabbed me. One hand curled around my back, the other headed to my ass, as he pressed himself to me. I loved it. I immediately scooted my arms up around his neck, and reached one hand to his soft, curly hair. He leaned in and kissed me, and of course he kissed me senseless, his tongue chasing mine, his warm mouth welcoming. Damn, he smelled clean and good. Damn, he looked good close up.

All of the things that I had been worrying about before he came over—tidying the house, setting the table, checking my makeup, generally fussing—evaporated.

"I've been wanting to do that for a while," he said in his sexy, husky voice, after he broke apart with a quiet groan. He pressed his forehead to mine, and looked at me, smiling. And it was like my brain went to voicemail.

Amelia's brain is out of service at this time. Please try your call again later.

I mustered a breathy response of "me too." He looked at me intently.

"Hi," he whispered, running his finger down my nose, and bopping it on the end.

"Hi," I whispered back.

He let me go, picked up the bags, sauntered into my kitchen, like he owned it, and started to take groceries out of the bags. "Can you arrange the flowers and I'll make dinner?"

I didn't know what I was expecting, but it wasn't this. That said, I'd take it.

"Sounds good to me." Sure, I would let him handle dinner. Did he want to clean my house for me too? WTF? Was he for real?

I pulled out a wide, low, clear, cylindrical vase for the white rosebuds, got some scissors, and cut the stems quite short so that they were even with the top of the vase. This made it a rather chic arrangement. Like I said, I gave good table. Then, I wrapped up the stems in newspaper, so that I wouldn't prick myself with the thorns.

"Thanks for the flowers," I said. "White roses are actually my favorite."

He grinned. "Lucky guess on my part. I like them, too." He walked over to the table, and inspected the vase. Turning to me, and running his finger down my cheek, he said, "They reminded me of you. You knew just what to do with them." He plucked a petal from one flower, and fingered it. I noticed that he touched the softness of the rose while I tried to avoid the thorns.

Deep thoughts, Amelia. Focus.

"So," I said brightly. "What did you bring?"

"Appetizers, wine, beer, and stuff to make chicken pasta and salad. Chocolate cake for dessert. Will that work?"

I was stunned, but this time not by his masculine beauty or damn gravitational pull, but how, um, perfect he was. My favorite flowers. Good food. Chocolate. And he was cooking. "Yep. That'll work." I aimed for nonchalance, and failed miserably.

"You hungry?" he asked.

I was actually ravenous but I shrugged. "A little." I didn't want to look too eager, abiding by another ancient girl law: never admit that you're actually hungry. He started rummaging around in my cabinets, and pulled out a platter. Then he pulled out cheese, crackers, and grapes from the brown paper bag and set them on the counter.

"What would you like to drink?" he asked.

"Beer is fine."

I pulled out an opener, handed it to him and he opened two beers, giving me one. Then he clinked his bottle with mine and took a pull. I must have looked at him a little warily, because he started reassuring me.

"Don't worry, I'm not going to jump you. I want to get to know you." He pulled out a knife from a drawer, a cutting board from my cabinet, and started slicing cheese, and arranging it with the crackers, on the platter. He washed the grapes, shook off the water, and set them on the side. Then he placed the snacks on the counter next to me and asked, "This okay?"

"More than," I muttered, truthfully.

"Open," he ordered, and popped a grape in my mouth.

I chewed, swallowed, and then laughed. "You really need to be shirtless and holding a fan when you do that again."

"Noted." He popped a grape into his own mouth, and made me a little plate, of cheese, crackers, and grapes. Then he made himself a little plate of the same, and started rummaging around for pans.

"Don't you want me to help you? I feel funny just sitting here."

"Nope. It's cool," he said firmly, leaving no room for argument. "I always liked cooking."

The awkwardness between us started to drop away. I nibbled on the cheese and crackers and grapes and drank my beer, while he chattered away about how his friend Yoda—I laughed at the name—taught him to cook, and how he loved Trader Joe's. "They have everything." He boiled water for pasta, sliced vegetables for salad and the pasta sauce, opened up jars of olives, and cut chicken. He told me about how busy the coffee shop was this week, and how he had a great time surfing that day, before he came over to my house. He used my olive oil, salt, and pepper, and cooked a chicken-olive-vegetable sauce for the pasta. He even had a wedge of Parmesan—the good stuff. He dressed the salad, put it in a bowl, and set out the chocolate cake on a plate.

In response to all of this, I shook my head with a small smile at his complete and total competence. He caught my look. "Restaurant business, Amelia," he explained.

"Were you ever a chef?"

"Nope. Just picked stuff up, mostly from Yoda."

While he cooked and stirred, he opened up a bottle of white wine and got out glasses, and set the salad on the table. I had set an elegant table, and when dinner was ready, we sat down. He pulled out my seat for me, put my freaking napkin in my freaking lap, and then went to get our dinner, which he had put on a platter to serve. It smelled heavenly.

I didn't know what I had done to deserve him, but I wasn't going to complain.

He sat himself, poured the wine, and handed me a glass. Then he raised his glass to me, but instead of a toast, he asked, "You know we went to high school together, right?"

I nodded. "I looked you up in my yearbook," I admitted.

"I've had a crush on you since then."

I was astonished. "Really?"

"Really," he confirmed with a devastating grin. "I wanted to date you since the moment I saw you, and I have dreamed about you since then. But the real you that I'm getting to know now, is so much more than the you back then, or the you of my imagination." Holy fuck. He wasn't scared to say how he felt.

"You were a freshman when I was a senior, right?"

"Yeah. So?"

"I don't want to feel like a cougar."

He laughed, a full male laugh. "I'm not one to tell you how to feel. You feel how you feel. I'm in this life to feel everything. Pleasure and pain. So feel how you feel, it's okay." Echoes of Christian Gray, my therapist. "That said, aren't we old enough for our ages not to matter?"

Wow. He was more mature than I thought. He was definitely more mature than me. He had this air about him, like he had figured out some truths about life. I smiled. "It doesn't bother me, if it doesn't bother you."

"Nope."

I learned, as dinner went on, that he was devoted to his younger sister. That he surfed almost every day. That he had surfed competitively but stopped. That he really loved Kona and roasting coffee beans in small batches. Then he admitted that he was a Harry Potter fan, and he liked Luna Lovegood the best. "Something about the moon," he muttered. This might work. As he talked, I found myself thinking that there might be more here than just me jumping his bones. I liked the guy. It was more than just physical attraction.

Relax, Amelia. This was a first date.

Once we got to the end of dinner, I felt happy and satisfied. A great dinner companion, he asked me questions, listened to the answers, talked about himself, and answered my questions. I loved finding out about him. He was so much more than a coffee shop surfer dude.

But still, the whole meal, all I wanted to do was crawl into his lap, take off his clothes, and get creative.

When I put down my wine glass at the end of dinner, I think he read the look on my face. "I'm not just a quick fuck, Amelia. Not with you. Not ever with you."

"Well, that's good to know," I said sarcastically, resorting to my usual habit of snark when I was faced with sincerity.

"You need to know something about me. I'm a sensualist."

I looked at him blankly.

"I explore pleasure," he explained patiently.

"Oh," I breathed, thoughts of sarcasm having vanished immediately.

"That means that I like to take my time. I like to feel things. I like to sense things. I like to explore. Can you handle that? Or are you the type who thinks that pleasure is bad?"

"Pleasure is bad," I repeated, semi-seriously.

He gave me a wicked grin.

"Let me see what I can do to convince you otherwise."

"But you're not going to do anything to me tonight?"

"No. Not because I don't want to, but because I do."

"That doesn't make sense. Can *I* jump *you?*"

He laughed. "Look, I'm not apologizing for what happened in the hallway at Southwinds. Fuck, that was hot. But I want to get to know you."

I had to keep myself from whining. "How long is this self-imposed moratorium?"

"Until tomorrow. I think I can hold out that long."

"So we're talking midnight, right? Lawyer here wants to know the parameters."

"Until midnight," he affirmed.

"Are you going to stay until then?"

He laughed. "If you want me to. We'll see how it goes. In the meanwhile, I may ask you to show me your Ollivander wand,

Hermione."

"Bastard," I muttered.

"What's something I need to know about you that you haven't told me?" He looked at me intently, open and curious.

"Isn't that a bit heavy for a first date?"

"Nope." He waited and shrugged. "No pressure."

"Well, I could tell you the story about how I've been clinically depressed for more than a year, and am on antidepressants that make it so that you're the first man to make me come in quite a while."

Okay. I could not believe that I just blurted that one out. I blamed it on the wine. And the fact that the damn Sun God made me actually feel comfortable. But this admission did not seem to faze him.

He looked at me, green eyes to blue, and said, "I want to know more about your depression, and what's happened to you, but you need to know that I'm up for any orgasm challenge you throw at me. Now, any interest in chocolate cake?"

TEN

Midnight

AT 8:33 P.M. BY THE TIME on the microwave, which I had determined was the fastest clock in the house, Ryan tugged on my earlobe gently. As I turned toward him, he slipped a fork, speared with a small bite of chocolate cake, into my parted lips. I must have made a moaning noise, because I caught him adjusting his pants.

At 9:05 p.m. he crouched down like a football player getting ready for a tackle, charged me, put his broad shoulder against my waist, hoisted me over his back like I weighed half of what I did, and carried me out of the kitchen, insisting that I was not to do the dishes tonight, despite my loud objection. I kicked and flailed and finally found purchase by holding on to his ass, heh heh. He threw me on the couch, and returned to the dishes, continuing our previous conversation.

At 9:06 p.m. I wandered back to the kitchen entrance hovering out of reach. Ryan walked over, touched the end of my nose with a finger covered in soap suds, and smirked, showing me his dimples.

At 9:22 p.m. he let his finger slip lazily down the side of my neck, as he helped me into my windbreaker.

At 9:26 p.m. he held my hand, while we walked around my neighborhood on the warm autumn evening, enjoying the Halloween decorations.

At 9:33 p.m. he continued to hold my hand, while we continued our walk.

At 10:03 p.m. he continued to hold my hand, as we walked up my walkway to my front door. He gave my hand a squeeze and released it so that I could unlock the door.

At 10:58 p.m. he brushed his fingers against mine, as he handed me a glass of sparkling water.

At 11:39 p.m. we both reached for the volume button on the music, at the same time, as we traded favorite bands on Spotify.

At 11:56:45 p.m. I had enough. I stood in the kitchen, a finger pointed in Ryan's handsome, freckled face, yelling at him, "You impossible man, you said you were not going to touch me until midnight, and you've been touching me all night long! I'm going to combust." It was all I could do not to stamp like a child. I was breathing hard, and trying not to show it, so I felt lightheaded.

He looked about the same way that I did, full lips separated, breathing shallow, curly hair messy from him running his hands through it during the evening. Then he gave me a provocative smile. "Just a few more minutes. Let's see how close we can get without touching."

"Bastard," I grumbled, and then I decided to take him up on his challenge. I stepped closer to him, so that we were facing each other, six inches apart.

He took a baby step forward, closing the distance between us in half.

I stepped forward an inch, and my knees and hands started to shake. My fingers twitched, itching to touch him. I licked my lips and he licked his. My toes stopped two inches away from his toes; my knees, two inches away from his knees; and my fingers, two inches away from his fingers. He looked down and I looked up, moving our faces two inches away from each other. He held his torso two inches away from mine, the whole way down his body.

Then he moved so that we were one inch apart. Everywhere. And then we breathed in and out, for two and a half minutes. The longest two and a half minutes of my life. His pupils dilated, and his cheek twitched. His attractive, clean mansmell washed over me. I felt his warm, sweet breath on my skin and I panted on him. He moved his finger and then stilled it.

And then the digital clock on the microwave changed to 12:00 p.m.

Midnight.

He abruptly lunged at me, palming my face with both of his hands, his long fingers probing my cheekbones, and pressed his full lips to mine, kissing me.

Then, just as abruptly, he pulled back, and looked at me closely.

"I wanna be gentle this time," he said softly, as if to himself.

"I don't," I retorted.

A low rumbling, deep in his throat, vibrated against my body, and he kissed me hard, again. Then, in a rush, he picked me up, one hand under my knees, the other under my neck, like he was a groom carrying me over the threshold, kissing me the entire way down the hall from the kitchen.

"Tough. This time will be gentle. Or at least as slow and gentle as I can go."

He carried me, at a clip, down to my bedroom, and eased me onto the bed, lingering, bending over me, and nibbling at my neck. He pressed back to stand up, and to turn on the light in the darkened room, and I said quickly, "Wait. No lights."

This was Rule #1. I didn't have sex in full light. Ever.

I could see the look on his face from the light in the hallway, and I knew that he knew that I didn't want the light on because I didn't want him to see my naked body.

Desperately, I tried to save the situation. "Ryan, let me light some candles."

He sighed. "Amelia, you are literally my wet dream fantasy from high school. I dreamt about you then, and I dream about you now. I want to see you. You don't need to hide. I already know your body is gorgeous," he cajoled.

"Please." I tried hard not to beg, but was spectacularly unsuccessful. Quickly, my mind racing, I came up with an excuse. "It's more romantic with candles."

I could tell that he saw through me, but he acquiesced with grace. "Where are the matches?"

He lit the candles, and I was pleased that I had managed to land on the truth: it was romantic. After he blew out the last match, he turned to me and looked at me, eyebrows furrowed.

"Do you want to go out with me next Friday night?"

That wasn't what I was expecting him to say.

He continued, "I don't want a one night stand with you. Will you agree to see me again after tonight?"

I nodded. "Yes." It was flattering that he wanted to see me again, but also exciting and soothing at the same time. Feelings! I was having feelings!

He seemed to relax, his shoulders lowering, letting out a breath. "Then I can take my time tonight, and we don't have to make our way through the encyclopedia from A to Z. More to look forward to."

I didn't know what he meant by an encyclopedia since I seemed to be stuck on "M" for missionary, by choice, but I felt relief that I wasn't going to be pushed entirely out of my limits tonight. "Oh-okay," I stuttered.

He came over to the side of the bed and stood there, looking down at me as I was sprawled, fully dressed, on my bed. He leaned down and pulled off one of my socks, and then the other, holding my feet firmly with his warm hands. This was strangely comforting. Then he reached down to the hem of my sweater and, as I helped him, he yanked it up over my head.

As he went to climb on the bed over me, I stopped him. "Nuh-uh. Yours too buddy. We stay the same amount of dressed."

He immediately unbuttoned his button-down removed it, and then tugged his white t-shirt over his head.

Holy Mary Mother of God.

The whole Irish-Catholic upbringing came in handy sometimes.

When I saw his chest before, at the beach, it looked hard and chiseled and covered with salt water from the ocean. When I felt his chest before, at the coffee shop, I could feel soft, warm skin, but

I couldn't see him under his shirt. Now I finally had the best of both worlds: vision and touch. *Yes.* I reached out to feel him as I gazed at all of the gorgeous planes of his torso. He climbed on the bed and straddled me, grinning down at me.

He stared at me for a moment, his knees by my hips, and then uttered, "*Fuck,*" emphatically, shaking his head a little. "I can't believe that I've got you here, under me, in bed. After all this time." He trailed his finger down my neck, down my shoulders, down my arms, and then over to my belly and up the other side. He softly brushed my breasts and then leaned down to kiss my neck, talking with his lips pressed against my skin. "It's a dream come true. What do you like? What drives you wild?"

I had no idea what he was talking about. "What do you mean?"

"Do you have any requests? I feel like I'm at a restaurant and everything on the menu is something I really want to eat. It's hard to choose."

I shook my head.

"Don't be embarrassed. No requests?" I shook my head again. "Fine. I'll order for the two of us." And he started to kiss his way down my torso, over my bra, down the middle of my belly, until he got to my jeans. With a quick flick of his fingers, he unbuttoned and unzipped them, and slid my pants over my hips and onto the ground.

I looked at him, and he grinned, knowing that I was going to demand that he take off his jeans. He got off the bed, unbuttoned, unzipped, and shucked off his pants too, showing me a raging erection barely encased by black Calvin Klein boxer briefs. The fabric contrasted against his tanned skin, lean waist, and narrow hips, and I could see his inguinal ligament, I'd learned the name of that one for sure, in sharp relief in the candlelight. Damn. Yum.

He reached behind me and unsnapped my bra so that all I was wearing was a tiny, pale pink, lacy thong.

"Now we're the same amount of dressed," he reported with a smirk.

"Not hardly," I started to say, but was caught off guard when he pounced. This time, he pressed his entire warm, hard, and soft body to mine, kissed me soundly, then kissed his way down my body, leading to my underwear. I rubbed my hands all over his hard ass, his strong back, his defined biceps, his veiny forearms, and his curly hair, as he made his way down.

His hands went under my ass on each side, and lifted me up. Then, down there, between my legs, he kissed me over my underwear, a hot, open mouthed kiss.

I convulsed.

My fucking brain decided to interrupt the pleasurable sensations of my body, and remind me that I didn't do oral sex. Ever.

But I really liked his hot breath on my skin and over my panties, and I wanted to see what it would be like. My need to follow the Rules clashed with the physical feelings of my body, each fighting for supremacy.

And then I realized that I trusted him. I had let him into my house and into my bedroom. I was letting him into my life. He was into me, no question—he told me so in more ways than one, and asked me out again. Besides being handsome, he was kind, and he looked out for me. And he cooked. I decided to open myself up and see if I liked it. With him.

The worst thing that would happen was that I didn't like it, right?

I'd just tell him, then. So, okay, easy decision.

I pushed my fingers through his hair, and he looked up at me from between my legs, and said in a husky voice, as if reading my mind, "If you don't want me to do something, that's fine. No question, I'll stop. I felt you tense. Are you okay with this? Because don't be scared. I'll make you feel good."

The truth seemed appropriate at this point. "I've never had a guy go, you know, down there."

He looked totally shocked, and opened his mouth to talk, but I beat him to it. "Madonna said that guys don't really like doing, um, what you're doing, or what you're thinking about maybe doing, as much as the romance novels say they do. She says it's just romance novel bullshit."

"Madonna has never been with me," he retorted. "I love it. Remember, I'm all about feeling. I'm the sensualist. Giving pleasure is one of the best ways to feel pleasure. I'm going to take my time and enjoy it. Give it a shot?"

Overwhelming words from a hottie. He really wanted to do this. Okay, then. I lost the power of speech but I could still nod, so I did.

Suddenly, I was dragged to the edge of the bed, my tiny panties hauled off, and his mouth nudged between my legs in my newly bare sex. I saw his golden, curly hair, and tanned upper back and shoulders between my thighs and knees. I really must look up the names of those muscles on his back because they deserved to be known by name. Just seeing him, kneeling off the bed between my legs, was so fucking sexy, I almost left my body and landed on the roof.

Before I could gather my wits, he was licking my already wet sex like it was his mission in life.

Oh my.

His tongue dipped and playfully touched. He alternated between sucking, rolling, and gently tracing me with the tip of his tongue. There must have been a million nerve endings down there and he was making friends with all of them. His head moved back for a minute, and one long finger slipped inside. Then two.

"You are so sweet, you smell so good, you are so wet, it's hard not to take you right now," he said, and sighed between my thighs, licking me again.

I lost the plot.

Basically, the entire evening had been five hours of barely-touching foreplay. I had enough and my body and brain were ready. He built me up with his fingers and his tongue, which took no time at all to my surprise, and then, oh my, I came crashing down.

I came. Hard. I saw stars. My mind was blank. Score another one for Ryan. But then it appeared that another one was on its heels.

No way.

But it was, and he rode it out with me, tasting, tonguing, and teasing me with his fingers. A prayer.

Dazed, when I came to, I looked down at him, as he looked up at me from between my legs, shit-eating grin on his face.

Correction.

Pussy-eating grin. He enjoyed that. Hmm.

Ohmigod. I just thought the word "pussy." Had I ever thought it before? It could be against a Rule I hadn't even come up with yet. I must have recovered, if my brain could argue with me like that. My fucking brain.

Before I fully came down from my orgasm, I noticed that he was now gloriously naked, and had magicked a condom out of somewhere and rolled it on to himself. He paused at my entrance, looking at me, looking right into my eyes, in the dim candlelight. His eyes seemed to warm and get bigger. Then he slowly slipped his huge, delicious cock into me, holding himself over me, his golden biceps bulging, his tan shoulder muscles popping, looking at me with his Sun God eyes.

He stayed there, seated in me, I thought, so that I could get used to him. He was, after all, a huge invasion. A welcome invasion, but still, an invasion.

And then he started to move, slowly at first. He bent his head down and kissed my neck as he started to move his hips faster. He slipped his finger between us and rubbed my clit insistently, but not roughly. My feet started to get hot from all of the blood flow to my extremities.

Then I could feel it building again.

Pleasure.

Intensity.

Traveling to the moon and the sun.

And with a soft shudder, I came again, feeling the spurt of pleasure in my brain and in my body. A few thrusts later, he shuddered as well and then relaxed into me.

ELEVEN

Rules

"**D**O YOU WANT ME TO GO HOME?" he asked. "I'd rather stay."
He lay next to me, naked still, our warm bodies under the covers, the lights all out in the house. He spooned at my back, his chin on my shoulder, his hands toying with my hair, while I looked out at the room.

I stiffened. No overnights. That's a Rule.

But I wanted him to stay.

"What's wrong?" he asked in a voice rough from sex.

"Nothing."

"Bullshit."

Of course he was right. I took a deep breath and let it out. Then I turned to him, searching for his gorgeous eyes in the darkness, then I ducked my head into him, tangling my legs with his, snuggling into his warm, broad chest, and nuzzling his pectoral muscles. I knew the name of those, for sure. I started kissing his torso, his nipples, and his soft skin covering strong muscles. I rested my chin on his chest and looked up, as he settled himself on his back.

"The truth? It scares me to be with you. It breaks all of my Rules," I admitted.

"What rules?" he asked, curious.

"I have Rules. About what I will or will not do in bed."

I could almost feel his eyebrows raising and his lips twitching. Bastard. He was going to laugh at me.

"Is this set of rules written down?" he asked in a mock-serious tone.

"No."

"Can you tell me what they are?"

Yeah, I could do that. Not.

"No."

"Can you text them to me?"

Okay, now he was just messing with me.

"Why don't I just text you the ones you've already broken."

"Nope. I want to know all of them, Amelia."

Fine. I'd tell him.

"I just don't do anything other than missionary."

He looked at me, bewildered, shaking his head once, quickly, back and forth.

"Um, what?"

"That's my Rule. I don't ever spend the night or have others spend the night. I don't go down on men and they don't go down on me. I don't do anything kinky."

This distracted him.

"What's kinky? I'm interested. Very."

"Everything but missionary."

He laughed, a low, surfer chuckle. "Okay. Nothing but missionary. I already broke that at Southwinds. Can I test your resolve on these rules? Am I allowed to encourage you to break them?"

Yes, I thought. *You already are. I was already trusting you like my therapist said to do. I was starting to feel things, and not just orgasms. I was starting to really recover from depression.*

I didn't tell him that. Instead, I said, "Fair enough," and smiled.

He wasn't letting go of the topic, though.

"Why do you have these rules?"

"Because." *Because everything else opens you up to trusting someone. Everything else makes you vulnerable. Everything else makes it so that you can't hide from someone. There was too much intimacy, and that scared me.*

"I'd never do anything that you didn't want me to do. And I'd never do anything to hurt you."

Not on purpose, I thought. I didn't say anything in response.

"Is that really how you want to be? Just missionary sex where you gamble whether you come, unless the guy really knows what he's doing?" How did he know that? For the first time, I wondered about his experience. He seemed to know what he was doing, for sure.

But he was being sincere, and I returned the favor. "Truthfully, I don't know what I want anymore. I just know that I like how you make me feel. I like how you make me feel things that I haven't felt in a long time. Like an orgasm," I said in a little voice. He squeezed me with his arms. "It was hard to have an orgasm while I took so many antidepressants. I'm still recovering. And I know that I am all confused."

"Let me straighten you out. If we come across a rule you don't want to break, you tell me and we won't break it. I'll listen to anything you want to tell me. Otherwise, let's just see where this goes. I'm never going to force you to do anything, but you have a shell, and I want to get in there and crack it wide open and show you how magnificent you already are, and how magnificent you'll be."

That statement would require some serious analysis when I was alone. So I moved on. "Not spending the night is one of my Rules. I don't do the walk of shame." Then I continued in a lower voice. "It's been awhile since anyone has wanted to spend the night here. I haven't been much company over the past year dealing with stuff."

"Would it bother you if I stayed?"

"No. I want you to stay here. It feels really good to have you here."

"Are you tired?" he asked.

"Not really," I said.

"Good, because I really want to fuck you again," he whispered in my ear. "I waited more than a decade to do it the first time." He traced my arm with his fingertips, making me have goose pimples up and down my body. I could feel behind me that he was getting aroused again. So was I. Still. I stiffened. I don't fuck.

"I don't fuck," I said.

He looked at me in amazement and curiosity, his eyes widening, and then narrowing in the dark. "Yes, you do."

"No, I don't." I was churlish and I didn't care.

He hauled me over him, having me straddle him, then pulled me down, gathered me in his arms, and asked, patiently and slowly, like he asked my order in the coffee shop, "Then what do you do?"

I immediately responded. "Have sex. Sometimes 'make love.' It's against my Rules to 'fuck.'"

"Newsflash, Movie Star, but I fucked you twice."

This might be true, if I admitted it. A part of me thought that I might be crossing another something off of my Rules. Still, I dug in and needed to fight for it. Lawyer instincts.

"I don't like that word," I groused.

"Okay," he said gently, "you don't like that word. But you sure seemed to like experiencing it. What other words don't you like?"

"What are you after now, a list?"

"Yeah, pretty much."

I could see that his eyes were dancing with amusement, and I decided to bury my face in his neck. Finally, I muttered, "The c-word."

He laughed out loud. "Cunt?"

I cringed. Then I took a deep breath and started listing. "Pussy. Cock. Dick. Vagina. Penis. Anus. Bitch. Semen." He was grinning. "Lubricant. I could keep going, if you like."

"Question. Is it that you think that you don't like a word or that you're scared of how the word makes you feel?"

I looked at him. "What are you, my therapist?"

"Not even close. But a word is just a word. You can make it mean whatever it is you want it to mean. You can award it whatever connotations you want to give it. But if you don't give it power, it doesn't have it."

I gazed at him in silence. So he was an enlightened sage, was he?

But he continued. "A priest told me that 'fuck' means to plow. So in the olden days you used to fuck a field. There's no reason to cringe about fucking. It's a normal word."

"A priest?" I asked.

"Parochial school," he said in explanation. "That's a story for another day."

"I like the word 'plow,'" I acknowledged.

"I like to plow you," he said, with a gravity-defying grin.

I gave him a shove.

"I really want to plow you again," he whispered in my ear. "Right now."

I took a deep breath, crossed another Rule off my list, got right up and personal with his gorgeous face, and said, with resignation, but also with a giggle, "Nah, just fuck me."

And so he did, again.

TWELVE

Feeling and Light

I AWOKE, WARM AND COMFORTABLE, with another heartbeat throbbing under my ear. In my bed. In the morning. Rule #7 (no spending the night), shattered, along with Rule #4, Clause 2 (no oral sex; rule broken for me, we'd have to see about him) and Rule #10 (I "make love" only).

Sheesh. What kind of lawyer was I? If I had myself as a client, I would have full-time employment to deal with all of my Rule-breaking.

You know what? In the soft, buttery Santa Barbara morning light, it didn't matter.

I yawned, snuggled into Ryan's chest, and looked up at him, content. He was already awake, his glossy eyes sleep-heavy, but intense. He had been watching me for a while, it seemed, as I slept on his torso, my legs intertwined with his. He shifted a finger from my lower back, trailed it up my spine to my jaw, and kept it there. And then he said the most beautiful words in the English language.

"I'll take you to breakfast."

At the restaurant, it felt like every female eye was on Ryan as we walked to our table. He was that good looking, sure, but it also seemed like there were flickers of recognition in their feminine eyes.

It made me wonder.

After breakfast, Ryan dropped me off at my house, saying that he had to go do some things that day for work, and that he had already scheduled himself at Southwinds every morning that week, but that he would pick me up on Friday at 5:30. He told me to wear "comfortable clothes" on Friday, kissed me breathless, and left.

I updated Marie, fended off Hugo by telling him about Ryan (he was immediately interested), and got ready for the week.

Ryan texted me late that night: *Sweet dreams.*

I wasn't sure that this was really my life.

Ryan texted me every day that week.

Monday
What rules do you still need to break?
Most of them.
Specifically?
Oral sex on you for one.
Ryan?
Crickets ...
Did not want to have to jack off at work today.
Sorry.
I'm not.

Tuesday

Another rule we need to break?

Nothing demeaning.

What does that mean?

Don't make me crawl naked across the room to you.

Don't give me ideas.

Would you want to do that? Can't believe I'm saying this but I'd consider it. For you.

Ryan?

Crickets …

Not specifically. I'm not into BDSM, although if you want to try, I'm up for it. The image of you, naked, crawling on the floor to me, totally submissive, totally turned on. Fuck. It might turn me into a dom.

[Giggles. Licks lips.]

Did not want to have to jack off at work today.

Sorry.

I'm not.

Wednesday

Hit me with today's rule that we need to break.

Do you have to go jack off?

It depends.

Well, I've already broke the no masturbation one today. For me, that is.

Ryan?

Crickets …

Fuck, woman.

On Wednesday, Hugo came to my office to take me to lunch, and chatted with Neveah, our receptionist. As Marie said, *that boy.* Still, they looked cute together.

Don't match make, Amelia.

Thursday

Send me a picture of your beautiful tits.

Send me a picture of your beautiful abs.

Your wish is my command.

Fucking hell, Ryan. Now I need to go break the no masturbation rule again.

Ryan?

Crickets …

Don't think I need the picture anymore.

Never mind. Yes I do.

Your wish is my command. Shit, I can't believe I'm doing this.

Ryan?

Crickets …

You are so fucking beautiful, Amelia. Did not want to have to jack off at work today.

Sorry.

I'm not.

Friday

Anything else on that list?

True doggy style.

Did not want to have to jack off at work today.

Anything else?

No toys.

Fuck, Amelia.

No dirty talk.

We'll see.

No anal.

Ryan?

Crickets …

Ryan?

Do not know why I torture myself.

Friday evening brought a tall blond surfer to my front door, his cool old truck looming behind him. I debated whether we should take my Mercedes, but decided not to be a bitch about it. He kissed me, grabbed my hand, and told me that I looked beautiful in my off-white sweater, fitted jeans, and flat brown boots. His long-sleeve, plaid flannel shirt stretched across his shoulders, and strained over his muscular arms.

Yeah, he was still the Sun God.

His truck was spotlessly clean.

He played me music as we left Santa Barbara, heading for a rural area just north of it. As we drove through the gates of a farm and down a dirt road, I realized that he was taking me to a country fair.

"A pumpkin patch?" I asked, incredulously. WTF?

"They have the best cider and doughnuts. I used to come here as a kid. It's only open this time of year. C'mon." We parked in a dirt parking lot, and headed for the fair.

The area was set up with food trucks, craft booths, a corn maze, rides, hay bales to sit on and for kids to climb, and pumpkins and gourds everywhere. It smelled like a fair, a combination of hay, cotton candy, burned butter, and grease from kiddie rides. A bluegrass band played in a shady area under a tree, with hay bales set up for seating benches. I giggled. I hadn't done anything like this in a long time.

Yet again, Ryan did the unexpected.

We held hands as Ryan paid for the entrance fee, and walked around looking at the arts and crafts. He bought us fresh pressed cider—pressed right in front of us, the apple peels squished into mash, hot apple doughnuts—made on a machine right in front of us, and tri tip sandwiches.

Yum.

We sat at a picnic table to eat and I noticed that when Ryan ate, he savored it, enjoying it. He ate slowly and carefully, licking the sugar from the doughnuts off of his fingers. It wasn't over the top or exaggerated; it was just an appreciation. We finished and explored the fair. When we walked past the petting zoo, he stopped. "Let's go in," he suggested.

"That's for kids," I protested.

"Are you allergic?"

"No."

"Then come on."

He paid a dollar for each of us to go in, and fifty cents for feed in a Dixie cup. We approached a 4-H kid holding baby chicks. Ryan reached for one and placed it in my hand, stroking it gently.

"Feel it, Amelia."

I dutifully petted the chick. He stepped behind me, wrapping his arms around my waist. "No, Amelia," he whispered in my ear. "I want you to remember how to feel pleasure, and not just when I fuck you in my bed. I told you, I'm a sensualist. Notice. I want you to feel how light the chick is, how soft its feathers are, how fast its heart races, how its claws dig into your skin." His full lips were so close to my ear, it was turning me on. He nibbled my neck, distracting me from the fact that I was standing with him on hay-covered ground, in an animal pen.

The downy chick was an adorable, little puff ball. Ryan was right. The little chick weighed almost nothing, but it felt so alive, so vibrant in my hands. Its heartbeat was nothing like the one I felt the other morning, with my ear plastered to Ryan's drool-worthy chest. I cooed at it, petted it, and gave it back to the 4-H attendant.

We met all of the animals in the petting zoo. It was funny, we towered over the little kids, out of place. Neither of us cared. I petted the goat with its weird, horizontal eyes, felt the rough bristle of the fat mother pig and her babies, and rubbed the back of my hand on a soft rabbit.

I was coming back to feeling.

After we visited all of the exhibits and booths, we went to leave. On our way out, Ryan grabbed a wheelbarrow, and started putting gourds and pumpkins in it of all sizes, colors, and shapes, the more bumpy and misshapen, the better. He insisted on buying a ridiculous amount of them, and hauled them to his truck, putting them in the back.

When we got back to my house, he set them up my walkway. Now my house was decorated like the others in my neighborhood. Wow. He was thoughtful. So, obviously, I invited him in. This was seriously one of the best dates of my life.

Fifteen minutes later

"Turn the light off, Ryan."

"I want to see your eyes when you come."

"You can see my eyes any old time. But I don't have sex in the light." I was naked, sitting on the bed, pulling up the sheet. I reached over and flipped the switch off.

He stared at me, confidence and disbelief radiating from him, as he stood to the side. He wore only boxer shorts, which made it a little hard to argue with him.

"No. Lights on," he ordered.

Scratch that. I was arguing with him. What the fuck was this? I was not going to play that game with him. I was in charge here. My Rules. My house. My body. No.

"No. Lights off," I snapped. He reached over and flipped the switch back on. I grabbed my shirt and went to put it back on.

"Lights off. Deal breaker."

He looked at me, grabbed my shirt back, and sputtered. "This is crazy. You are beautiful. Why do you need to be in pitch blackness?"

"I just do, okay."

"You're not letting me in."

"It's early," I hurled the words at him. "I've let you in more than anyone else. I don't do it in the light."

Holding me by my waist, he dragged me to him. "What is this?" he asked in a quiet voice. Probing. Gentle. Damn him.

"I can't do the light. No light. It's against my Rules." I behaved stubbornly and I knew it and I didn't care.

"So the Rules protect you? Do they really do that?" His voice was sharper now, challenging me.

I had had it.

"Yes!" I yelled. "They do." I glared at him. I wasn't backing down from this. I tried to cover myself up with the sheet.

I had no idea what he was going to do next. Was he going to back down? Was he going to face me head on? How big was this fight going to be? I was a lawyer. I could do the head on challenge. I was stubborn too. I could sulk with the best of them. But what he did next completely undid me.

He prowled towards me, put his hand under my jaw, and caressed me with his golden fingertips. Talk about an about face. He then leaned in and kissed me softly on my lips.

"You beautiful thing," he murmured.

"I don't understand why you can't understand why I need the light off."

He let out a breath and sighed. "Let's try something," he said gently. "Stand here. Take a deep breath." All lights were on and he was still ordering me around. I was not going to be fucking obedient. Not going there.

Right?

But something about his tone made me trust him. I dropped the sheet that I was clutching, and walked to the middle of my bedroom, wearing nothing.

I had been naked with him before, but this felt different, because I felt more exposed and vulnerable. Indeed, I had never felt more naked, standing there, in my bedroom in my little house, all the lights on, in front of a man. This man. I felt like all of my flaws, my scars, especially that one, were on display.

I stood there and waited, while he looked at me. His eyes passed over my entire body, starting with my head and moving slowly over me, all the way down to my toes. I could see the hunger in them. I braced to protect myself. I wanted to move my arms, to cover my breasts, my abs, my scar.

"I want you to understand something, Amelia. There is one thing about you that I want you to change."

I was immediately disheartened and slumped my shoulders down. What was it? My abs? My boobs? Did I need to make more money? Dress differently? Get a new job?

"I want you to stop being so hard on yourself. I want you to accept yourself."

I looked at him in stunned silence. The fuck? So he *had* been talking to my therapist.

"Everything about you, physically and mentally, is beautiful. Your insecurities are beautiful. But you don't need them." He circled me, trailing a finger around my waist as he surveyed me. "Let me point out some things that I adore." His fingers teased across my head. "Your dark hair. It smells like hot girl. I love to feel it, play with it. I love it when it's up and I really love it when you take it down."

I shrugged in embarrassment and looked away from him.

"Your beautiful face. You have the face of a movie star. I've never seen eyes like yours on anyone else. Your eyebrows and cheekbones make you look so elegant. Your lips make me think that they need to be on my body at all times. Especially around my cock." He grinned suggestively. "Your ears, your neck are stunning. Everything that goes on inside your head is attractive. Your intelligence. Your humor."

I looked at him, stunned, as he continued to list all of my attributes, touching each, caressing each.

"This hollow, right here, on your collarbone. Priceless." He stalked to my back and ran his tongue from the nape of my neck to my ass. "This backbone. It's where it's at—you've got spirit, and one hell of a backbone, but it's also superb. These curves." He took both hands and whispered them down my sides, from my armpits to my hips. "I've never seen such impressive curves. You are all woman, Amelia."

"Isn't that just a nice way of saying that I'm fat?"

"You're not listening," he chided, "so I'm gonna keep going until I get this into your head." He reached towards my front and gently caressed a breast in each hand, pressing his boner into my back. "These are fantastic tits. Fucking fantastic. They are the stuff that make hard-ons happen, obviously." He kept one hand on a breast, kneading it, and took the other hand down to my belly button. He splayed his hand over my belly. I covered his hand with mine. "This right here, is so soft. It's like nothing you know. Soft skin. It's womanly, comforting. It's so attractive."

He walked around in front of me and kneeled.

As an aside, I'd never had a man kneel in front of me. My ex proposed to me over the phone, the asshole. But I heartily recommend having a guy kneel in front of you. Wow. Talk about sexy submission.

Focus, Amelia. He was worshiping you.

I waited for him to continue.

But then he traced my C-section scar first with his finger, and then his tongue, and looked up at me, imploring.

"I know you've had a baby. You can tell me about it when you're ready. This scar is part of you and it means that you're a woman. It's gorgeous and meaningful and I want to kiss it as often as I can."

I burst into tears.

"I'm gonna keep going and then I'll hold you as long as you need.

This pussy. I'm not good with words, but I could write, like, a poem about your pussy." He grinned. Still kneeling, he kissed one hipbone and then another. "Your hipbones and hips are fantastic. And your ass. Another poem." He reached around and caressed my ass, while pulling his tongue out and getting a few licks into my pussy. His fingers trailed down each of my legs. "You have knockout legs, Amelia. I love to look at them. I love them wrapped around me. They're so hot."

And I was sobbing.

I'd never had anyone go through my body, inch by inch, and tell me that it's acceptable. But he didn't just tell me that it was acceptable, he told me it was wonderful. Attractive. Attractive to the Sun God. I'd never felt the affection that he just gave me.

I didn't feel naked and vulnerable anymore; I felt cared for. This fast, he had got through yet another one of my defenses: my insecurity. While I had tried to tell myself that I was a badass, in reality I never believed it. And not believing it was precaution against getting hurt. If I took myself down first, no one else could do it, and no one could do it better than me.

He trailed his fingers from my ankles up to my hips, then with a graceful movement, got up off of his knees. He traced his fingers up my sides, over my shoulders, and around my back, then down to my ass again. Then he moved his warm hands to my back, and hugged me hard, kissing the top of my head.

I fell into his embrace, sobbing, getting tears all over his naked chest. I didn't care if I turned red and my eyes got puffy. I didn't care anymore whether he saw my C-section scar or my Buddha belly. I didn't care anymore that the light was on.

All I cared was that I finally felt accepted, not just by him, but by myself. By telling me that he accepted my body, exactly as it was, no changes, with my history, gave me permission to loosen the grip of unconscious self-loathing that being in the dark symbolized. He broke me open, telling me that he saw me in the light, and he liked it. Because of that, I felt better in my own skin.

THIRTEEN

Sabrina

M Y SOBS SUBSIDED. I WAS A WET, puffy mess. I shivered. Ryan's chest glistened, completely soaked in my tears. I looked up at him and burst into laughter. "I didn't mean to drown you. I'll get a towel."

"I have a better idea."

He clasped my hand, and pulled me down the hall into my little vintage-tiled bathroom. With a flick, he turned on the bath, like he had done it a million times before at my house, which he clearly hadn't. While the water filled up, he looked down at me and smiled. "Let's warm you up, and get you relaxed."

That's a very good idea. After being so emotionally wrecked, there was no way that I was up for energetic sex—at least not right now. But I still wanted to touch him, to hold him, and have him hold me.

Maybe this was intimacy, I thought.

He held my hands, as I slipped into the bath, and then he took off his boxer shorts and stepped into the water behind me. I nestled into him, my back pressed against his awesome chest, his strong calves around mine, and his arms around my waist.

Wow.

This was a comfortable place to be. My very own personal Sun God, in my bathtub. Radiating warmth.

As I leaned against him, he put his chin on my shoulder and teased my ear with his lips. I let out a deep sigh and felt myself start to relax.

"Ryan," I said in a low voice.

"Yeah," he muttered, biting my neck, little nibbles. Little amazing nibbles.

They say that bravery is feeling the fear and doing it anyway. So I decided to be brave. "I want to tell you what happened to me."

He continued to nibble my neck. "I'm listening."

"But I don't want you to run away screaming."

He released my torso, and turned me around by my shoulders, so that he could look me in the eyes, a serious expression on his face. "There is nothing that you could tell me that would make me not want you. I've had a crush on you for a decade. Whatever you tell me is not going to change that," he said with utter sincerity.

Whoa. Okay, then.

I had only told my story to Marie, Hugo, and my therapist. But everything that Ryan did made me feel like it was safe to trust him. *This was vulnerability.* I recognized it, and I was going to try it and see how it fit me. I knew that I could get hurt. It was a risk. But I had already been hurt before, and closing up really hadn't helped me. It was time to try something different. So I took a deep breath and started talking.

"As you know, I was the prom queen and I dated the football quarterback in high school."

"Jonathan Sanchez?" asked Ryan.

Fuck. He knew who the asshole was. Of course he would. Soldiering on.

"Yeah. He wasn't my first boyfriend. I dated others in high school, but I dated him my senior year and then followed him to Boston for college. The short story is that once we got there, we fought, we broke up, we dated others, but then we got back together. After a while, we were inseparable. It felt inevitable that we would be together forever."

Ryan traced his hands up and down my arms, with light, soft strokes, while I talked.

"Looking back on it now, with what I know now, it was a pairing of convenience. It wasn't love, although back then I thought it was. It wasn't. It was just like we were supposed to be together, and had been together for so long, and knew each other for so long, that we were just, together. Without questioning it.

"It's not dramatic. I don't think he cheated on me. I don't think he had it in him. But now, looking back on it, he was so cold. I know now that he wasn't a good lover. He wasn't engaged with me. He didn't question my Rules. We did it missionary position. He gave me orgasms with his fingers, which I thought was good sex. But I don't know if it was me keeping a part of myself from him, or him keeping a part from me, but neither one of us was truly open with the other. I knew that sex could be good. I knew what an orgasm felt like. But I didn't trust him. Not really."

"He never pushed you on your rules?"

"Never."

He uttered something under his breath that sounded like, "He didn't deserve you."

"So after we got back together in college, I continued at Harvard for law school, and he went to Boston University for medical school. We studied long hours, and barely saw each other. My parents approved of him. He's from a good Catholic home. My mom loved that. His parents are doctors. My dad's a doctor. They all knew each other for ages. It was all arranged. I was in love, or so I thought. So when he called me to ask me to marry him, I agreed."

The hands on my arms stilled. "He asked you to marry him over the phone?"

"Yeah. Romantic," I said sarcastically.

"No," he said emphatically, "it's not. More like a business merger."

"We had the perfect wedding. Three hundred people there. My parents announced it in the paper. They spent so much money on it, it was like a fairy tale. We had a gorgeous honeymoon in Bora Bora. It's totally cliché. Then we got back to California, bought a house, and went on with our lives. He opened up a medical practice in Los Angeles, and I worked for a mega firm in Century City. I worked all the time and I hated it. I knew that I had to put my time in, and make my way up the chain of command of the law firm. But I also knew that I wanted more. I wanted a child. I wanted a family.

"He told me that he wanted a child too, but that he wanted to wait until we were more settled. I agreed, because I was fine with that. It seemed like we were on the same page. A few years later, he agreed to start trying, and within a few months, I was pregnant.

"I was so excited. So happy. I was going to scale back my hours, and try to be both a lawyer and a mom. I didn't know how I was going to do it, but I was going to take every minute of maternity leave offered, and I was going to be a good mom.

"Well, we got bad news after one of my doctor's appointments. My baby had Down's syndrome. Not only that but she had other problems. Heart problems. She was unlikely to survive the pregnancy, and she was unlikely to live very long if she did survive the pregnancy. I was hoping against hope that she would live, and I was reading everything I could about Down's syndrome, happy to have a child."

He stilled. I ignored him and kept going, determined to get the story all out.

"I wanted to keep her." I whispered. "He wanted to terminate the pregnancy."

His arms tightened around me.

"It was my baby. Our baby. A wanted baby. No way was I terminating the pregnancy. He didn't want the baby. He didn't want our baby."

I fought back the tears that were welling up again.

"He was a doctor. I couldn't believe he wanted to terminate his own daughter. We fought all the time. The stress was no good for my pregnancy. He couldn't stand to be around me. We couldn't stand the sight of each other."

"If you want to stop, you can," said Ryan gently.

"No," I said determinately, "I'm going to finish this. So, I have an asshole husband who doesn't love me, and doesn't agree with me. I have a fantasy dream life, destroyed. And I have a baby growing inside me who is going to have special needs, and isn't likely to live very long. I filed for divorce in my sixth month of pregnancy, when it became clear ... when it became clear that I deserved better. I left and moved up here to Santa Barbara. I continued my pregnancy by myself, with my best friend, Marie, coming with me to my appointments. He wanted nothing to do with me, and nothing to do with our child.

"In the seventh, almost eighth month of pregnancy, I took a turn for the worse. I was admitted to the hospital on bed rest, with constant monitoring. I had to have an emergency C-section or both of us would die."

Tears streamed down my face and I started to sob, again.

"I still have nightmares about the emergency C-section. The gurney. The lights. Being rushed into the operating room. So they cut her out, and I didn't get to hold her. She was so tiny. She only weighed ... ." I broke off. "She was so small. They whisked her away immediately. But then she was in the NICU and I could only touch her through the incubator. But she was suffering. The heart condition was too much for her. She lived six days.

"The coffin was the smallest I have ever seen."

I couldn't go any further. He wrapped me in a bear hug as I sobbed. "What was her name?" he asked quietly.

"Sabrina Michelle Sanchez." After a bit, I stopped crying. "There's more." I felt him nod. "I didn't recover from this. My postpartum depression got worse and worse until I was suicidal. I didn't really come close to doing it, but I had overwhelming thoughts of suicide. And those scared me so much. Marie, she saved me. She got me help." I turned around and looked at him. "So I'm a mess. My history is a mess."

We stayed in the bath in silence for what felt like a long time.

"Yeah. I can't fix that," he whispered. "Guys, we like to fix things. We like to make things better. We like to take action. This, this is part of you. It can't be fixed. But you need to know that I think that you're the bravest and strongest woman I have ever met. And the most beautiful, inside and out."

"You still want to be with me?"

I said it as a joke, but I was really scared of what his answer would be.

"Of course," he replied. "You want me to make love to you?"

I stilled at his words. Not "fucking." "Making love." Now he was following my Rules. Or was he?

I thought about it. Yeah. I did. I nodded.

He helped me to stand up, then pulled me out of the cooling bath water. He wrapped a towel low around his hips, looking like an ad for shaving cream, and dried me off with a towel. Then he wrapped me up in one, with my arms pinned to my sides, like a swaddled baby.

Then he crashed his lips into mine and kissed me, a passionate, wet, soulful, hungry kiss.

He led me to my bedroom, where, holding my hands, and looking at me in the eyes, with the lights on, he made love to me, until we both surrendered.

I felt clean and spare, like I had been filleted down to my bones, and was starting to rebuild my muscle with good things.

FOURTEEN

You're Gonna Need a Dress

I PUT MY COFFEE CUP DOWN on the counter.

"Ryan, how come you can come over to my house and make better coffee than me, using the exact same equipment and coffee beans as me?"

"Magic, Hermione."

I harrumphed in response. It was too early in the morning for me, although Ryan seemed to be a morning person. I suppose he had to be, working in a coffee shop.

He picked up his keys, wallet, and phone to leave and put them in his pocket. Then he wrapped me in his arms in a crazy bear hug, enveloping me in his warmth, kissing my hair and inhaling me. I curled my arms around his narrow waist, and stuck my hands in the back pockets of his jeans, feeling the hard muscles of his fantastic ass.

I didn't want him to leave. Not at all.

"Come over to my house this week," he commanded, talking against the top of my head. "On Wednesday. I can't wait until the weekend. I want to have you in my bed. I want to break some more of your rules. I want to break the record for the number of orgasms you've had in one night."

I automatically shivered in anticipation. What would it be like to have orgasms delivered by Ryan on his home turf? I took a moment to review my work schedule for the upcoming week in my head; Yes! I could spend the night on Wednesday. I was getting to the point where I wanted to spend every minute with him, because he was getting to be more than just a sexy surfer to me. Something much, much more. I needed to analyze that thought at a later point in time, too.

But he was still bossy, and I needed to call him on that.

"Are you asking me or telling me?" I shot back at him. Of course I was just messing with him; I was really curious about where he lived, and I was glad to be invited. Although I was fearful that it was some crummy bachelor pad, based on the cleanliness of his truck, and the way he did the dishes, I hoped that it would be tolerable.

"A little of both," he said warmly, dimples appearing on his beautiful face. "Mostly telling."

Dimples.

I lost my train of thought.

Focus.

Then my train of thought got back on the rails. He was still telling me what to do. If I was truthful, I would admit that his bossiness made me wet. But I still had a backbone and a pathological need to push back.

"You're a short boarder, right?" I had seen him at the beach with a short board.

"Yeah," he answered, a little warily. "Why?"

"You're this weird combination of confident bastard and mellow Zen. You competed in surfing, so you clearly wanted to win, but surfing is a mellow, natural, individual sport that doesn't require competition. It's like you're an Alpha male hippie."

This brought out a chuckle. "You nailed me."

"No," I argued, "I think you nailed me."

He laughed. More dimples. Damn. In a low, husky voice, he murmured, "And I intend to do so every chance I can."

When he talked to me like this, I couldn't handle it. It was like he was breaking me into dirty talk. I know there is dirtier talk than this, and I'm not sure why I resisted it, but I wanted to keep pushing back at him. I opened my eyes and looked at him. "So you're in charge here?"

"Pretty much," he said, lazily trailing the tip of his tongue against my jaw.

I was starting to forget why I was protesting. I continued, "You order me around—or at least you try to—but you are also really into allowing me to do what I want and letting me do what I need to do."

"Yeah, that sounds about right," he agreed easily, now biting my ear with little nips and nibbles, and making me moan.

"Well then. I'm glad we agree," I ended lamely.

He looked me in the eyes and kissed me with an open-mouthed, full-blown, hot-as-hell kiss, then broke apart and commanded, "Wednesday."

I let out my breath and nodded. He was just so bossy. The thing was, I liked it. Weird. Having him take charge felt hot, along with a strange feeling of relief and excitement, but it sure shot my feminist cred out the window.

Fuck my feminist cred.

Ryan went to the door and paused, looking at me. He looked at me with wide, green eyes and asked, "Another thing. What are you doing on Friday night?"

I have to say that it was not a turn off for him to constantly ask me out. Unlike Hugo or even Jake, with Ryan, I wanted it.

"I don't know. Why?" Now it was my turn to be wary.

"Do you want to go with me to a business dinner? It's for a work charity. I have to go, my company sponsors it. I'm not sure you're into those types of things. I really want you to come, though."

He had shifted gears from bossy Alpha male to imploring. He was just so cute. Plus, I was good with business dinners. I normally liked these type of things because I liked getting all dressed up.

"Sure," I replied immediately.

"You're gonna need a dress. I'm warning you, I'm gonna wear a tux. It's black tie."

I was temporarily distracted by thoughts of Ryan in a tuxedo. Sunny, golden curls and handsome face, topping broad shoulders, in a suit jacket, leading to his bulging biceps, leading down his body, to his lean abs, in a white shirt, tucked into suit pants, which led to, yeah.

Mental image impressed.

That would do.

Then he asked, "Do you want me to get you a dress?"

I laughed. That was a strange question, and sort of sweet. "No, I can get myself a fancy dress, thanks."

He took my hand, pulled me into the entire length of his hard body, kissed me again, taking his time and having his tongue do a Lewis and Clark exploration in my mouth. After he got me all bothered, he took off in his old truck. Men, I thought, exasperated. Just when he got me all, you know, he left.

No.

Just this man. This is the only man who gets me so keyed up. I skipped into my room, hyped from the kiss and from the anticipation of my upcoming week, and called Marie, ignoring the warmth pooling in my sex. Now it was time to shop.

Monday morning at work, I talked with my mom. She was the kind of mom who went to church every morning to say the rosary. I love my mom; she's patient and kind. I knew that she cared for me and wanted the best for me. But she could be extremely meddlesome, and she was ultra-conservative and religious. I didn't mind these things in other people. I just wasn't conservative or religious. Still, after a lot of therapy sessions, I was realizing that I was undergoing something called "individualization." I was starting to be my own person. It was a work in progress.

I had hoped to cut her off at the pass and used the "I've been busy with work, Mom," standard line, which was also normally the truth. But no, not this time. She was on to something.

"What's this I hear from Marie's mother?" she asked, beginning to press my buttons.

Oh fuck.

Because Marie and I have been friends since third grade, our mothers have also been friends since we were in the third grade. This meant that, of course, Marie told her mom that we had gone shopping and, of course, her mom told my mom that I had a date. I should have known that word would get out. Or, I should have sworn Marie to secrecy.

Here was another thing about my mom: she was the original snob. Word got out that I was dating a guy I met in a coffee shop and she didn't like it. I mean, I was a snob too and the princess was the prodigy of the queen, but I was trying to change that, and change myself. This time I got angry. I needed to defend my man, if Ryan was indeed "my man."

"Mom, it doesn't matter what his income level is, or what he does. He is the kindest man that I've ever met."

We had more words and then I hung up the phone on her, still angry.

Fuck.

I would have to call her later and apologize. Christian told me that where you are from does not determine who you are. I still loved my mom, but I remembered that she was not me.

On Wednesday morning, Jake stopped by my office, his hunky body taking up the whole doorway. "I need you to stay tonight and work on the evidentiary objections to the motion for summary judgment." This was the life of a lawyer. Guess I didn't get to check out Ryan's pad after all. At least not tonight. I called Ryan.

"Sorry, I have to work late tonight. Rain check on seeing your place?"

"No problem. I'll see you Friday. I'll pick you up at six."

Friday evening, I showered slowly and carefully, shaving everything. After, I lubed up with lotion, used my perfect scent, and fussed over my hair, letting it be down and in waves. I put on heavier eye makeup than I usually did.

I put on my dress. Marie and I had found a great satin dress, in a "sheen green" color from Crayola. Look it up. It was strapless, and the bodice folded over at the top, hugged my curves, with a matching belt at the waist, and then went straight down. Since my ass was not straight, I made the dress curvy. It was the kind of dress Ava Gardner would wear with gloves above her elbows, while dripping in diamonds. Since it was about sixty years too late to wear gloves, I didn't. Instead, I wore strappy, silver heels and earrings with three diamonds hanging in a row connected by platinum chains. They were the nicest ones I owned.

I liked how I looked.

Thinking about the narrowness of the skirt of my dress, I was wondering how I was going to get this dress into Ryan's truck, and figured that I'd offer him my Mercedes. Still, by the time he knocked, I was ready. I'd never been the type to make a guy wait, so I figured that I wouldn't start now. I picked up my silver envelope clutch that held my phone, an ID, twenty dollars, and my lipstick, grabbed my keys, and opened the door.

I was breathless.

Ryan stood there in a tuxedo, a classic tuxedo. His tan face and curly hair contrasted with the crisp bright white of his shirt. He wore a black tie, his jacket was buttoned up, and his shoes were shiny. I loved the stripe going down the side of his pants. As usual, he smelled clean and fresh, but manly.

"You look gorgeous," I managed.

"I could say the same for you," he replied, and kissed me on the cheek. "I really want to mess up your lipstick, but I imagine that you might kill me."

"You're right. I would kill you," I agreed, not meaning it in the slightest.

He smiled at me, unabashedly looking me up and down. Then he shook his head and held out his hand for me to follow him. "You look so fucking sexy, Amelia. Thanks for coming."

I locked my door, and he led me down the path to a shiny, black Tesla. "Where's your truck?"

"Not the type of night for a truck," he said. "Thought this would be better." I figured that he'd borrowed it from a friend, and I didn't ask any more questions, not wanting him to feel bad. I wondered how much the tux rental had set him back. They certainly did a good job measuring him. There was no indication that this was a rental. He must have picked a nice place.

"So where are we going?"

"Bacara." Ooh boy. I had been to Bacara once before for a business lunch, and you couldn't get two ham sandwiches and two ice teas for less than a hundred bucks. I should have brought more than twenty dollars in my purse.

"Wow. That's posh."

He looked over to me and smiled. "It's a fundraiser for a charity that my parents started. If you have it at a nice place, the people who need to be there to donate will come with their wallets open."

"What kind of charity?"

"Cancer research. I lost my dad to cancer, my mom to a ski accident. Both while I was in high school."

I was aghast. "I am so sorry." Why didn't I know this? Hadn't I asked him any questions about himself? He had told me so much about himself, but I realized that he had not told me much about his history. I couldn't imagine losing both of your parents while you were in high school.

"I had to grow up pretty quickly. But I carry on their traditions and this is one of them." We drove in the quiet Tesla, no music playing, and I appreciated its comfortable interior. It wasn't that far of a drive to the luxurious Bacara hotel, and soon enough we pulled into the resort, and a valet approached. Ryan handed the valet his keys, and came around to escort me out and down to the ballroom where the event was.

I saw a sign that said "FIELDING PHARMACEUTICALS FOUNDATION" with an arrow pointing to the event area, which was decorated with white orchids everywhere. Like I thought. Posh.

And then I realized.

Fielding Pharmaceuticals.

Fielding.

Ryan Fielding.

Ohmigod.

He was an heir to the Fielding fortune.

I was such an idiot.

In awe, I looked at him again. He wasn't a surf bum or a coffee shop manager. He was a mogul.

"Shall we?" he asked, giving me an admiring look, as he held out his arm to lead me into an area with people dressed in tuxedos and gowns, jewelry everywhere and waiters circulating with champagne glasses. Trembling, I didn't know what to do. Normally I could handle these types of events, but now I felt completely stupid.

I wasn't the one slumming with him; he was slumming with me.

FIFTEEN

Exorcism

I TURNED TO RYAN.

"I need you to fuck me. Right fucking now," I exhaled.

His body stiffened, and he looked at me in surprise. Then he started to grin, but looked me in the eyes and looked concerned, his eyebrows furrowing, his jaw set. "Do you want the coat closet or do you want me to get a room?"

I loved that he didn't question it.

"Either, Ryan. Now." I ordered.

He grabbed my hand and pulled me to the check-in desk. "We need a suite," he demanded.

"Yes, Mr. Fielding," smiled the obsequious male employee, who started to type on a computer. Of course they fucking knew him at Bacara. The employee continued, "That will be-"

"It doesn't matter," Ryan cut him off and handed the employee a black AMEX credit card (why hadn't I noticed it before?) and signed the check-in form. The employee handed him two keys, and then Ryan grabbed my hand, and pulled me to the elevator.

The elevator opened immediately, and he hauled me inside, then pushed me to the walls, pressing his hard body against mine.

"What the fuck, Amelia? Are you okay?"

"No. No, I'm not. I need you to fuck it out of me."

"Fuck what out of me?"

"That I'm a fucking snob."

He shook his head slightly, and looked adorably confused. "What?"

"I thought you were a coffee shop manager."

"I am a coffee shop manager."

"But you're Ryan Fielding. Everyone knows about Fielding Pharmaceuticals. I had no idea you were related."

"So?" he challenged.

"You're completely out of my class."

He pulled back, his face looking thunderous. "What the fuck is that supposed to mean?"

"Do you own that coffee shop?"

"Yeah. I own ten, and I'm working on franchising them."

"Then why are you working the counter and wiping down tables and driving around a beat up old truck, for fuck's sake?" I yell-whispered.

The elevator door opened. He grabbed my hand and pulled me down the hall. I was practically running in my heels to keep up with him. He opened the door, hauled me in, and closed the door, then slammed me up against it. He didn't turn on the light and I didn't bother to look at the room. I only saw him. He glared at me, his body pressed to mine, fury emanating from him.

"Slowly, now, so that I understand. What. The. Fuck. Is. Going. On?" he demanded.

"I thought you were just a surf bum and a coffee shop manager. I'm totally attracted to you, but I thought ... I thought ... I'm such a bitch ...." I trailed off.

"You thought I was lower than you," he hissed.

I really didn't want him to know that was what I'd thought of him. But I wasn't going to lie. Time for the truth. "Yeah," I admitted.

He pulled away from me with a growl, turning away. Then he looked back at me, his face pained. "What does money have to do with anything?"

"I'm sorry. It's the way I was raised. It's everything to my parents. In fact, my mom found out I was seeing you, and tried to get me to stop." He looked incredulous. "Obviously I stuck up for you, and told her she was wrong. But still, there was this part of me who was, who was ... ." I couldn't finish that sentence. "So now I come here and I find out that you've been hiding all of this from me," I continued, gesturing around the room.

"What, exactly, did I hide from you?" he asked, dripping with venom.

"That you're way out of my league."

"I'm not. I didn't hide anything from you. I invited you to my house, for God's sake."

"Where do you live?"

"Faria Beach, on PCH." It figured that he lived on Pacific Coast Highway, the ocean-front location of world-class real estate. A shack cost two million dollars. I shook my head. "Honestly, Amelia, I figured that since you looked me up, and knew that I went to high school with you, that you Googled me." I shook my head in response.

"Is there a Wikipedia article about you?"

"Yes. I figured that you'd already read it, since you Google everything."

Fuck. Completely out of character, I hadn't Googled him. We stared at each other.

"Is this a reason not to see me?" he asked, still pissed. "My money?" he spat out.

I paused.

"No." But then I went on. "But you're not who I thought you were."

"I'm exactly who you thought I was," Ryan argued back. "Nothing's changed." He looked me in the eyes and, after a moment, when he spoke again, his voice softened. "You really didn't know, did you?"

"No," I said, quietly.

"I'm so used to people knowing who I am and wanting me for my money, I just assume—" he began.

"I assumed, too. We were both wrong, I think. I think I just learned a lesson about not jumping to conclusions about someone."

"I'm not going to hide it, I'm pissed at you, Amelia. What the fuck are you thinking about money and class and shit like that for? Isn't the only thing that matters whether we like each other, and whether we make each other happy?"

"You're totally right." I felt contrite. "I'm an asshole. I don't deserve you."

"Stop it." He took a deep breath, let it out, and looked down at me. "First fight, huh? Well, I wasn't expecting tonight to be one for a fight."

He gave me an ironic smile.

"That makes two of us," I muttered. "So what do we do now?"

"I just want to be with you. I couldn't give a rat's ass what happens downstairs. I can make excuses if I need to."

"Do you have to give a speech?"

He looked away. "Yeah."

"Fuck. When?"

"Not until after dinner. Look, you're more important. Are you ready to go back down? Do you need to chill here for a while? Do you need me to fuck you?"

"Door number three," I whispered.

"Yeah, me too," he whispered back. And then a change came over him, and he went into Ryan-Alpha-hot-guy-in-control mode. "Come on. I don't want to mess up your hair too much, it's too pretty, so we're going to do this this way." Now that I looked around, I was in the most incredible hotel room I'd ever been in. A luxury suite, tastefully decorated in soothing beiges and modern furniture, with more rooms than I could see. "Keep those sexy as fuck shoes on. I'm going to bend you over the bed, and fuck the bitch-snob out of you. Deal?" I nodded. "I need to hear you say it."

"Deal" I said, more strongly. "Make me forget that I ever thought less of you."

We went into one of the bedrooms—there were two!—and he pressed me into the bed, breasts crushed against the mattress, ass in the air, still fully clothed.

"I'm going to mess you up a little bit, but not too much. You're just too hot, your gorgeous ass in this dress. I had to fight getting hard, seeing you." He lifted up the skirt of my dress, way up over my hips and waist, and put his face on my lower back, kissing me softly. Then he hooked his fingers in both sides of my panties and put his teeth on the waistband of my panties, peeling them slowly off of me with his fingers and his teeth, his nose trailing down my lower back, my butt crack, and between my legs, as I stepped out of them. I looked back, and he had shrugged out of his tuxedo jacket, and flung it on an armchair.

He knelt between my legs, pushing them way apart, and licked his way up my leg, pausing to suck on the back of my knee, and then traced his tongue up my inner thigh to my pussy.

So now I was calling it "my pussy." Progress.

My ass up in the air, his face between my cheeks, he began to lick and suck my pussy in his dominant, giving, way. He fondled my butt then slipped a finger into my pussy, as he licked my clit, my legs spread wide, my face pushed into the bed. This was what I needed.

"Oh, fuck yes. *Yes.*"

He built me up quickly, my sensitive nerve endings singing as he licked and caressed me with his tongue and fingered me with expertise.

It built.

It built some more.

It built even more.

Sensations, pleasure, feeling, tension, and more pleasure, all built, centered on the activity of his tongue, that man between my legs.

Then I came, a full and complete release of all the tension, all the crap, all of my mistakes, my scream muffled by the bedspread. I released my ignorance, my bitchiness, and my colossal error in judgment about this awesome guy.

In a flash, he had unbuttoned his tuxedo pants, lowered his zipper, adjusted his boxers, and released his cock, rolling a condom on.

Yes.

Quickly, he filled me up from behind with his huge cock. This time, he didn't wait for me to get used to the size of him within me, just started thrusting as I came down from my orgasm. As was my custom with Ryan, I lost the ability to process rational thought. All I was doing was feeling. I was in the moment, feeling pleasure, feeling the delicious pain of him hitting me up at my womb (or wherever in my body the tip of his penis hit), feeling him go in and out, in and out. I was glorying in the connection with this amazing man.

"Oh, fuck me, you are so wet. This is so hot. You are so goddamned beautiful, I'm going to come so hard." He kept up a kind of muttered dirty diatribe, as he thrust and thrust into me.

This was fucking, no question about it. Rutting. He was not making love to me. Even though we were in a classy place, partially dressed in classy clothes, this was baser stuff. He got me off, and now he was getting off.

But the thing was, I loved it. It was a monumental connection with him. I turned him on, he turned me on, but we also were creating something new here. His hands were braced against the bed, fucking me thoroughly, without apology. Even though he wasn't stimulating my clit, I could feel an orgasm coming.

Fucking hell.

I had never, never, never had an orgasm through penetrative sex alone. I'd never come without someone, or me, stimulating my clit on the outside.

But something about Ryan hitting the inside walls of my pussy, there's that word again, must have really hit the right spot, because

I started to convulse again. This time my orgasm was sweeter, more surprising, and more intense than ever before. Ever, in my life. It was a different feeling, a different sort of orgasm, more natural and organic, unforced, and overwhelming. With every quick, hard thrust of his cock, he stimulated the right spot. Boy, it was like he hit a trigger on a reaction that I never knew I could have.

I came. Again. Just by his cock stimulating the right spot.

This time I completely came apart, uninhibited. I screamed, I clenched the sheets and released them, my arms and legs were completely useless, and I felt amazing.

Ryan thrust a few more times and, his dick impossibly huge within me, he shuddered. I actually felt the warmth of his cum within the condom. He collapsed on my back, breathing hard. I was breathing hard too.

We just lay there for a while, our breathing strained, until it eventually regulated. He pulled my hair out of the way, nuzzled my neck, and said hoarsely, "Wow."

"Yeah. Wow. I think you fucked not only the snob out of me, but also the bitch, and you may have even exorcised the princess too."

"I like the princess," he said against my neck. "The snob and the bitch, eh, I'm fine with, but if you wanted an exorcism of them via fucking, I'm happy to have been the one to do it."

He pulled out of me and pushed up, pulling off the condom and heading into the bathroom. "Be right back."

I shoved my face in the bedspread, and took a deep breath. I couldn't move, but I sure felt better.

SIXTEEN

Stuck in the Middle with You

FIFTEEN MINUTES LATER, WE LEFT the suite to rejoin the charity dinner downstairs. We both looked a little flushed, me more than Ryan, but we were mostly put back together. I certainly felt calmer. Ryan held my hand lightly.

The seaside Bacara resort was beautiful, with Moorish style architecture and expansive grounds, an indoor-outdoor facility, comfortable year round. We walked to the ballroom for the reception and checked in at the table outside the room, receiving our table assignments: *Mr. Fielding and Ms. Crowley, Table 1.* Of course, we were at the first table in the front of the room, in the middle. The table of honor.

I didn't know how many people were there. Hundreds? A lot. Everyone was dressed up and holding elegant drink glasses, chatting, listening to music, and bidding on a silent auction. Apparently we had not missed the event entirely with our interlude.

We made our way through the crowd to get to our assigned table, so that I could set down my purse, and I learned that we were seated with the key note speaker, a prominent oncologist, and the President of the Fielding Pharmaceuticals Foundation, along with their families.

Ryan held my seat out for me, and I took it. Then he pushed it in for me. Now I knew why he had such elegant manners; he was used to it.

"Would you like a drink?"

I nodded. "White wine."

"Okay," he said, "I'll be back."

He headed to the bar, through the crowd. Although there were people milling around everywhere, because, as I now knew, he was a local celebrity, the crowd parted, and people stared at him everywhere he went. The reaction of the crowd was not just because of his height, his masculine beauty, and the grace of his lean, muscular body. He had a presence. Yes, he was tall and handsome, but he also had a magnetism that made people want to look at him. They got out of his way.

A few people stopped him on his way to the bar to shake his hand, and he was genial and friendly. I watched him as he waited in line for our drinks.

While I waited, I looked at the program for the dinner. I almost gasped when I learned that this was a $2,500-a-plate dinner.

Yes. I was way out of my league.

I turned around and looked at who was around me. There were lots of people, mostly older, chatting and enjoying themselves. Right behind me, at the adjacent table, sat a group of four women, all stunning supermodel types, who were talking loudly among themselves and watching people cattily. They were all wearing barely-there dresses, with major jewelry and designer heels, sipping wine. Since it was California, they were uniformly blonde, tan, and leggy. Ugh. Save me from the Botox. I wondered about their dates and whether they had escaped just in time.

Then I heard one of them mention Ryan's name.

"He called me a few months ago," Blonde Number One said. "I didn't call him back. I probably should have, but I didn't want to be too available for him."

Blonde Number Two, without lowering her voice, said, "I can't believe Ryan brought that fat woman as his date. I wonder if he has any standards anymore."

I reddened. This was not happening. This was not happening. Bitches. I did not understand the need for women—especially genetically gifted women—to bring other women down.

Just ignore them, I told myself. Their opinion didn't matter. No one could make you feel inferior without your consent. Yeah, I was resorting to Eleanor Roosevelt.

"She looked old enough to be his mother."

Oh, for fuck's sake.

Blonde Number Three giggled, a hard, ugly giggle. "He probably used his 'I'm a sensualist' line on her." She continued, in a low, sexy imitation of a male voice, "'I'll show you pleasure and we'll experience the sensations of just being.' Or some shit like that. He's such a whore. Didn't he cheat on you too, Tiffany?"

For the second time that night, I was hit in the solar plexus. Was Ryan not sincere with me? Was his pleasure-sensualist-feeling bullshit just a line that he used on everyone?

And cheating? No. Not with me.

It felt so real, everything with him. He seemed so sincere.

But was I in denial? It fucking hurt to feel like just another one of his conquests. I mean, I figured he had experience, but to be faced with it, live and in person? This was a nightmare, and not the type that I could wake up from.

Despite the fact that I knew that I shouldn't go there, I shouldn't let them in, I shouldn't give their evil comments any validity, I went there. My thoughts dove straight to hell.

He could have anyone he wanted. Why would he need to cheat? Was he going to cheat on me? He knew my secrets. Was he going to use them against me? Was I going to get hurt worse than I already was?

So what should I do? I had already freaked out on him once tonight. He solved that with a very expensive fuck. Should I confront him about this? Should I just ignore it and let it go?

My brain, already the source of my depression and problems, started slipping into its old pattern of numbing things out. I tried to talk rationally to myself. Perhaps I was getting ahead of myself. We had not talked about our relationship, whatever it is. We had not agreed to be exclusive. We had not formalized anything. There was just his "you're with me" command in the hallway at Southwinds.

Had he ever taken any of them there?

Toxic thoughts, Amelia.

And then my thoughts went worse. Had he cooked for them? Knelt before them, worshiping them? Woke up with them?

I waited, quiet at the table, for Ryan to get back with my wine.

I saw him waiting in an extremely long line and I wanted him back because I was so uncomfortable in my thoughts, and feeling very alone.

And then I saw him.

My ex, Jonathan.

This was the date from hell, no fault of mine, no fault of Ryan.

Shit, fuck, shit.

I needed to leave and I was trapped, at the front of a crowded ballroom, with bitches to the side of me and my rat bastard ex-husband by the doors. And I'd apparently been brought here by someone with quite a line.

I couldn't help but hum the song, "Stuck in the Middle with You." But I wasn't sure if I had Ryan at my side. I wasn't sure of anything.

Fuck.

Then, with my sick sense of humor, I remembered. That song was used in Quentin Tarantino's violent classic movie, *Reservoir Dogs*, when one of the characters was getting his ear cut off. It occurred to me that getting my ear cut off might be less painful than feeling what I was feeling at that time.

The depressive, dangerous, and suicidal thoughts bubbled up for the first time in weeks. This was what I got for letting myself feel, for letting myself be vulnerable and open: nothing but pain. Darkness. Dark thoughts. Fuck, not this again.

I had come so far and no, I couldn't control my brain any more. It wasn't working. It was like a record player needle had slipped into the groove in the vinyl and I couldn't get it out again.

I shouldn't be here.

I shouldn't exist.

There was nothing in this life for me.

I began to hyperventilate.

The room spun. My only thought became, I must leave.

Trying not to call attention to myself, I got up from the table, my hands trembling, my legs about to give way, my body shaking, and headed to the door, Jonathan be damned. I needed some fresh air. I needed to think. I needed to not think bad thoughts. All the blood rushed from my face and I felt like I was going to faint, yet again.

I pressed through the crowd, although no one seemed to really look at me. I made it out of the ballroom, and headed down the corridor to the bluff outside by the ocean. Lights from boats and oil derricks twinkled out in the evening over the water. The evening air woke me up a little bit, but I was starting to numb out. I stared at the ocean and the activity beyond, not processing, just looking. And then I heard—

"Amelia!"

It was Ryan. He was running, full bore, in a tuxedo, curly hair flopping, after me.

After me.

While I watched him run, a bit detached, my body reacted and I realized something: he made my heart beat faster. Every single time I saw him, he made my heart beat faster. And here, running after me? I didn't know if my heart could take it.

I spotted a bench and took it, sitting, grateful to have solid support for my body, and fresh air to breathe.

"Hey, are you okay?" he asked, barely breathing hard. Fit bastard.

"Yeah, I'm fine," I lied.

"No you're not. Talk to me. Do you want some water?"

I looked at him dazedly. I didn't know what I wanted.

"I'm getting you some water. Stay here."

He slipped away quickly and was back in two seconds with some ice water that he must have taken off of a table. I drank it gratefully. Sitting down next to me, he just studied my face, not taking my hand or touching me. Then he asked, quietly, "What happened in there?"

I didn't know how to respond to that question. After a while, I managed to say, "I can't go back in there."

"Why not?" he asked immediately. I came up with a ready excuse, among the many I could choose from.

"My ex-husband is in there." *And there were gorgeous women verbally beating me up. And you may be lying to me about wanting to be with me. You might not mean what you say. You might be a philanderer. I might be just another woman you have had in bed, and I want to be more because you have shown me so much more, already. You have challenged me, you have worshiped me, you have held me, and you have cracked me open, and you've convinced me that there was something sweet and vulnerable inside me, and that it was safe for me to show it to you. You have woken me up and you have made my heart beat inside my body, which used to be a grey, empty shell. I was feeling alive with you.*

And then I realized that the cruel words from the beautiful bitches hurt so much, because I was starting to have major feelings for Ryan, beyond just sexual feelings.

If I could admit it to myself, I could fall in love with him.

And having his sincerity questioned so flippantly, so teasingly, so recklessly hurt. It really, really hurt. Fucking brutal.

Especially since I had spent the past few years shutting myself off from feeling anything. With depression, I was too scared to feel anything, so I felt nothing. Recently, opening myself up, I was starting to feel all of the range of emotions, both good and bad. But now, these bad feelings? They felt like they were going to destroy me, eat me up from the inside and make me a hollow shell that would never feel again, ever.

I felt unsafe and utterly alone, even though his warmth was right by my side.

After a moment, I finished the water, and handed the glass back to Ryan, who put it down on the ground and looked at me hard.

"Your ex-husband is here? Why?"

"Probably because he's a doctor."

To my surprise, Ryan grinned at me, a lopsided, cutie boy grin, and grabbed me with a "C'mere," putting his arms around my bare shoulders. What I wouldn't do for that grin. His warmth always made me feel better. His physical body heat, his hot kisses, his giving personality. It didn't solve anything, but it made me stop having this extreme, physical reaction to all that had just happened.

"Not looking forward to seeing him. So this night isn't what either you or I had hoped," he said lightly.

Despite the panoply of dark thoughts I'd had in the last few moments, I laughed. "No, I suppose not. You're not who I thought you were. My ex-husband is here to torment me." *There were beautiful bitches, with apparent carnal knowledge of you, cutting me with verbal knives.*

"Do you want to go back in there, Movie Star, or do you want to stay out here?"

"Stay with me out here for now, and then I'll go back inside."

"Deal," he said immediately.

Then I backtracked. "I didn't mean to be so clingy, if you need to go inside—"

"You're my date, Amelia. I care about you. I'm not going to let you fend for yourself, especially not with an evil ex-husband on the loose."

He cared about me.

What did I do with that? Did I just accept it at face value? Did I read into it and over-analyze it, based on what the beautiful bitches said?

He smiled at me, his warm face lighting up, and drawing me in. He sat with me for a long time, my head in the nook of his arm, holding me.

Then, once I had calmed my breathing and relaxed, he stood, held out his hand, and clasped mine, confidently, walking hand in hand back to the swanky party.

To recap the evening:

I learned that my crush slash sort-of boyfriend was actually an heir to a major fortune.

I had the life-altering realization that I was a complete and total bitch for thinking anything about him at all, except for who he was for real—not a surf bum or a coffee shop guy or a mogul, but just Ryan, down-to-earth, mellow, and sensuous. I knew now that whether he had money, or whether he did not have money, he was hot, thoughtful, and sexy, and got my pulse going. I didn't need to judge him any other way, and I needed to get the voice in my head that said otherwise to just shut the fuck up.

My ex-husband made an appearance. Asshole.

I didn't know what to think about those bitches who said that

Ryan was insincere and a cheater. That made me question whether I really knew him at all, even if I had finally understood that his money—whether he had it or didn't have it—didn't matter.

And, finally, I needed to think about the fact that I might just be falling in love with my surfer.

I was so confused and had been hurt too many times that evening. I had been hurt too many fucking times in my life. I didn't know what to think or believe anymore. It was overwhelming. Everything I had thought was wrong. I needed to make up my own mind on what to believe, but I had no idea what the right way was to do that. So what did I do?

I drank.

A lot.

SEVENTEEN

A Drunk Amelia is a Funny Amelia

First glass of wine

RYAN WALKED ME OVER TO the table, pulled out my chair for me, and pushed me in, acting now very gentleman-like and formal in his tuxedo, after he had unceremoniously fucked me, and then ran after me in it. Still, he somehow managed to look unflappable. That was a little annoying, really. He handed me my glass of wine and gave me a big kiss on the mouth, before he sat himself next to me.

I could hear the tittering of the females next to me. A new determination came over me, however, and I was heartened by the public kiss.

Tough, bitches. He was mine.

Maybe.

The seat beside me was unoccupied, and while Ryan talked

animatedly with the couple next to him, after polite introductions, I nursed my glass and had time to think.

This was the most uncomfortable public event ever. I looked like a fucked up mess. My fancy dress didn't hide the recent orgasm or my multiple freak outs this evening. I had cleaned up in the posh bathroom a little bit, but still, I was sure that the reapplication of makeup did not hide my flushed face or my unnaturally bright eyes.

I felt so strange, so many different emotions at once. Too many for a depressive to handle. I downed my wine with a gulp and Ryan refilled it with a bottle on the table.

Second glass of wine

Ryan was some sort of multi-millionaire. As in hundred millions or something like that—Fielding Pharmaceuticals had developed several potentially successful cancer treatments, and had been sold to a larger drug company years ago. It continued to operate as a research and development division of that corporation. And I don't know why this made such a difference, but it did. There was something about having that much money. He could do whatever he wanted. And it gave him some power. So I needed to rearrange my thinking about our relationship.

Regardless, there was no bitch-snob anymore. I was not going to let there be one. And, feeling the second glass of wine, I grabbed Ryan by the lapel and whispered in his ear, "There is no more bitch-snob, Ryan."

He looked at me with amusement. "Good." He bopped my nose, looked me in the eyes for another beat, and then went back to the conversation with the muckety-muck on his side.

"Do you see how he is with her?" I heard one of the blondes say.

I hitched up the bodice of my dress and gulped another sip of my wine. I don't think Ryan heard her because he was monopolized by the grand marshal of the event.

I poured myself another glass of wine. The food should probably start to come soon.

Third glass of wine

I made it through a discussion with the keynote speaker, who was sitting next to me, asking me about my law practice. I made it through watching the keynote speaker get up and talk. I wasn't totally sure what was said, however, and probably wouldn't have paid attention even if I were sober.

Fourth glass of wine

Ryan, glorious and handsome, stood up at the podium, thanking everyone for coming, and imploring them to open up their wallets for the Foundation. As he spoke, he caught my eye, and he looked at me intently, a grin on his face in front of everyone.

Fifth glass of wine

I don't remember what happened, sorry.

Next bottle of wine

I stumbled out to the hallway, looking for the restroom, teetering on my heels. Lights overhead spun, and the walls moved. Or maybe it was me who was moving. With tunnel vision—in a hallway like a tunnel—I made it to the bathroom and came back. As I went to go into the ballroom again, there was Jonathan, my handsome, but now slightly gone-to-pot ex-football player ex-husband.

"Amelia," he said, grabbing the tops of my arms, as I almost fell into him.

"Zzzshjonathan," I slurred.

"Wow," he said, getting a look at me. "How drunk are you?"

"None of your bizzz-nezzz," I retorted, weaving a little bit to shrug out of his grasp.

He raised his eyebrows, as if to say oooooh-kay, and turned to leave. One of the blonde society bitches from the table next to us, who had been trashing everyone all night long, came up to him. "Jonathan," she purred. "I wanted to talk with you." Ugh. They hadn't been sitting together. Apparently he knew her.

He turned to go with her, and then looked at me, shaking his head. "I wondered what happened to you," he said. "Now I know. Get ahold of yourself, you're an embarrassment."

And in my drunken stupor, I lunged at him, making a fist and slamming it into his cheekbone.

Fuck, that hurt.

He looked at me, squinting his eyes, and hissed, "Get help."

Second shot of tequila
And I remembered no more.

Later
"All patients need to be strip-searched. It's protocol."
"But I'm an attorney. I'm a professional."
"No exceptions."

"But I thought I could check out at any time. This is voluntary. There's no 5150 hold on me. I don't have anything with me."

"We need you to remove all of your clothes, and place them on the bed. While you are here, you cannot have any shoelaces, drawstrings, or underwire in your bra. Do you understand?"

"But I don't want to take off my clothes."

"This is procedure. A female nurse will be in here to do your assessment. She will be looking for cuts and other markings on you. You can wear this gown, but leave the ties open."

The brusque male nurse left.

I stood, locked in a room that defined the term "institutional." It was straight out of a movie about the loony bin. There's nothing in it but a wooden bed with a mattress that had a sheet on it. No electric plugs, no furniture, no pictures, there was nothing else in this room except the fluorescent light overhead and a large door with a window. The door locked on the outside, but not on the inside. I'd never been in a room with nothing else in it, except when moving into or out of a home. It was so, so eerie.

I could not leave this room. If I wanted to go crazy and climb the walls, I could. If I wanted to scream, this was the place to do it. If I wanted to pitch a fit and show them that I really belonged in a mental institution, now was the time to do it. Something about the bare walls made me feel like I could hear the echoes of past mental patients' screaming embedded in them.

I did not like this room. At all.

But I needed to get help.

I needed to stop thinking about killing myself. I needed to stop planning to kill myself. I needed help.

I needed to take a deep breath and get on with it.

156 | Leslie McAdam

I looked in the adjacent bathroom. If I was being facetious, I would call it an "en suite." There were no locks. There were no door handles. The door could not close shut.

I had never been in a bathroom with a door that intentionally never closed.

No towels, no towel rack, no toilet paper rack, no trash can, no soap dish, no soap. Nothing but a sink, toilet, and toilet paper sitting on the tank.

So this was a mental institution bathroom.

I removed my clothes and placed them neatly on the bed. I put on the hospital gown and waited for the nurse to come in.

It took a long time.

The nurse came into the room and told me to open my gown.

She had a clipboard in her hand and stared at me, naked, taking notes. I didn't have any cuts on my body. I didn't have any tattoos or piercings. She saw my C-section scar even though it was healed by now. As healed as it would ever be, that is. I didn't try to kill myself with anything other than my thoughts and a railroad track. I turned around and showed her my back.

It was embarrassing for someone to see me naked. In the light.

She silently made notes on her clipboard. Then she picked up every piece of my carefully folded clothes, and felt each item all the way through. She confiscated my bra, because it had underwire. She told me that I could get dressed, and left the room.

I took a deep breath. This was the first step to getting better.

EIGHTEEN

Exclusive

IOPENED MY EYES AND BLINKED, confused. Upon waking, I found myself in a huge, extremely comfortable bed, my head on top of several soft, white pillows, my body covered by a fluffy, white duvet. Sunlight streamed into the room, bathing it entirely with bright, clear light. I lay all alone in a silly-huge bedroom. It seemed to take up an entire floor of the house, with floor-to-ceiling windows on three sides.

How drunk did I get last night?

I had never been here before, not even in my dreams. Looking around, I realized that I had no idea where I was. I really hoped that this was Ryan's place, because if it wasn't, I'd hunt him down and kill him for leaving me alone with someone who'd kidnap me and take me to an ...

... awesome beach house. Yeah, this must be Ryan's home.

Swinging one bare leg over the side of the bed, and then the other, I learned that I was wearing some sort of white surfer t-shirt that I'd never seen before. It went down to the tops of my thighs. If Ryan put this on me ...

... then he was the sweetest guy ever. How much of a perv was he when he took off my clothes? Sheesh, that's a thought for another time.

I caught a glimpse of myself in the reflection of the window. Holy rat's nest, Batman. And what was I thinking going to sleep with makeup on? The black smudges around my eyes meant that I must look like Catwoman, too. Shit. I needed to find a bathroom, and fast.

But before I did, I couldn't help but gape at the view beyond my reflection in the window.

The entire Pacific Ocean stretched out like a moving blue-green blanket, taking up most of the view. If I looked to my left, I could see a bit of the coast that stretched down south to Ventura, and eventually reached Los Angeles and beyond. But if I looked straight out, all I saw was water. It was so soothing and so beautiful.

But more soothing than the view was the sound. The open windows let in the cool air, which felt comfortable and moist. The waves provided a constant noise, drawing back, and then folding into the shore. Drawing back, and then folding into the shore. Pause, crash. Pause, crash. It made you feel like you were a part of something infinite, looking at the endless waves like that.

Deep thoughts, Amelia. Get a move on.

Taking a tentative step onto the cool-to-the-touch, dark wood, wide-plank flooring, I quickly scurried to what I hoped was the bathroom. I chose correctly, if you could call a room the size of a second house, a bathroom. A huge two person—*two person*—shower dominated the corner, floor to ceiling windows on two sides. Talk about a view. I had no idea that Ryan indulged so much. Okay, so probably no one could see him shower from up here—they would have to be out on a boat with binoculars.

Hmm. Ideas. Shit, now I was the perv. Then I had further ideas about joining him in the shower. Just some good, clean, fun. I turned and saw a sunken bath tub that could hold, what, twelve people? Geez, did he have orgies in here? I really wanted to try out the sunken tub. Fucking decadent bastard. Well, that's not fair to him, he was so down-to-earth, normally. But his bathroom was over-the-top.

It took me a full minute to work up the guts to finally look at myself in the mirror, but when I did, it wasn't that bad. I cleaned up the makeup that had smeared, tried to tame my hair, and made myself at least a little bit better for morning perusal by the Sun God. Now it was time to explore. I felt a little shy, honestly. Where was he?

I left the bathroom, crossed the bedroom, and headed to the door on the opposite side, hoping that it was an exit, just as Ryan bounded up the stairs and into the bedroom, a latte in one hand and a cup of black coffee in the other, miraculously not spilling a drop. Show off.

Oh, yeah, and he was shirtless, glowing, in dark blue-and-white, Hawaiian flower-print surf trunks that were so low on his hips I thought he could get arrested, his abs and happy trail on full display. That's my man.

Wait, was he my man?

Well, that thought could wait until after coffee.

He smiled his huge smile and said, "Morning. I figured you'd want some coffee." He held both cups in his hands, bent down and kissed me chastely, and then handed me the latte, keeping the black coffee for himself.

"You figured right," I agreed gratefully and took a sip. My own personal Southwinds coffee maker. It was times like this that I felt lucky to be alive. Such a change from last night.

"Need Gatorade? Advil?"

Surprisingly, I didn't. I remember Ryan ordering me to drink water all night. That must have saved me from Hangover City. I gave him a small smile. "Not now. Thanks for taking care of me last night."

Ryan cocked his head to one side. "It was my pleasure." Then he continued, suggestively, "More than you know."

I immediately panicked and my eyes popped open. "What did I do? I mean, after I hit Jonathan?"

He laughed. "Relax. Nothing happened after I found you holding your fist, except that you had a few too many drinks and were a quiet, happy drunk who fell asleep in the car on the ride home. Scout's honor."

"Not even when you undressed me?"

"Does copping a feel count?"

I thought about it. "No."

"Then no, nothing happened." It was nice to hear that validated. I thought that I could trust him, but still, it felt nice to have my trust in him confirmed after it took a hiding behind the woodshed last night. I was going to have to talk to him about the blonde bitches.

After coffee.

"Come on over here." Ryan took me to the other side of the room, where there was an indoor-outdoor terrace. It had glass doors that you could close off or open, depending on the weather. He kept them closed, likely because I was only wearing a t-shirt, and we sat on adjacent chairs, our feet up on the coffee table, drinking coffee in silence and being comfortable with each other, watching the waves.

After a while, we finished our coffee, still half-dressed. The waves were lulling me back to sleep, and I was just thinking that it sounded like a good idea to curl up in my surfer's arms, when he started talking.

"What else freaked you out last night?" he asked in his sexy, husky voice. The one that made me not function properly. It still was a form of voodoo, I thought. But my recovery time was getting faster.

"What do you mean?"

"By my count, you freaked out, first, when you figured out that I'm not a slacker, but I have a couple bucks in the bank, and, second, that you saw your asshole ex-husband, who had a bad date with your fist. But I thought that you were freaked about something else too. Dunno what."

I expelled a breath of air. He was more perceptive than I gave him credit for. Fuck. Do I bring it up? Or do I let it go.

It was probably the better thing to base a relationship, or whatever this was, on honesty, not on hiding. I had hidden from everyone for a long time, so this was going to be another brave step for me. But no way was I going to tell him that I was falling in love with him. Nuh-uh. At least not yet.

For now, though, I sideswiped the issue and blatantly changed the subject. "So you have a Tesla, huh? Then why do you drive the truck?"

"It was my grandfather's truck, and ended up being my dad's first truck. Living out here at the beach, I have to take extra good care of it so that it won't rust, but I love it. It's great for surfing. The Tesla is better, you know, for the earth, seeing as how it is electric, but I am attached to that old truck. But you changed the subject." He looked at me pointedly.

God, he was perfect.

Okay, decision made. I was going to be brave and talk to him about it.

"There were these women next to me at the dinner tables, while you were getting the drinks."

"Yeah?"

I took a deep breath.

"Which part do you want first?"

He leaned back. "There's more than one part?"

"Yeah."

"Whatever you want, Movie Star, I'm listening."

"Well, first they called me fat and old."

He immediately got angry. "Fucking bitches. That's why I hate this society shit. I only do it because of what happened to my parents."

A small knot in my stomach, which I had been previously unaware of, relaxed. I knew I shouldn't be surprised that he took my side, but truthfully, I was. Maybe this was the depression talking still. I tried to hide it with bravado. "Yeah, that's what I thought." But then I couldn't help but ask him, "You don't think I'm fat and old, right? I mean, we've gone over this, but it sucked to hear it out of a stranger's mouth."

He looked me straight in the eyes, green to violet, and said, "You have the body of a goddess and you are the perfect age for me. I'm twenty-eight, you're thirty-one. Big deal. After we talk, I will remind you of how beautiful I think you are, in every way. And what do they mean, old? How old were they? Did I know them?"

Well. "They seemed to know you. Intimately."

He furrowed his eyebrows, thinking. "Where were they sitting?"

"Right next to us, to the right as you looked at the stage."

"Fuck. I know who you are talking about. A bunch of boring, shallow blondes?"

I looked at him and thought, *you're the guy who puts on charity functions in honor of your parents. You're the one who drives your dad's first truck. You're the one who cooks me dinner, who makes me feel whole, who takes care of me. You're the opposite of shallow.*

You're not the guy who picks up blondes by the half dozen.

"Yeah."

"That's Tiffany and Destiny and a couple others. They go to every charity event, and want to be in every damn issue of the Santa Barbara society pages. They use me, I use them. I'm sorry if it sounds bad, but sometimes I've needed a date and they're low-hanging fruit."

"That's pretty cold."

He tilted his head to the side.

"They don't mean anything. Not like you."

Okay, that was ... amazing.

"I feel like I am opening up with you, I'm being vulnerable with you, but ..." I trailed off and tried again. "I feel like I'm exposing myself to you, but it's not reciprocal. It was a huge shock to find out that your parents had died. I don't know what you—"

"I'll tell you. I'm not going to hide anything from you. Ever. I told you, I'm a sensualist, I live in the moment. I live for pleasure and I live for the now. I do it while surfing. I do it while fucking." He gave me a teasing, knowing smile. "I do it while *making love*. I do it when I work on my business. I could care less about all this stuff," he said, gesturing to his home. "I could care less about the money. I'm a fifty-one percent shareholder of Fielding Pharmaceuticals, along with my sister. It's a publicly traded company. But I care more about building up a good, local coffee shop business, and possibly franchising it than about Fielding Pharma. Southwinds is a business that is actually mine. I lose myself when I go to Kona and talk with the farmers, pick the coffee beans, make the roasts."

He paused and looked at me intensely. "I lose myself when I spend time with you. It makes me forget that I'm an orphan. It lets me block out the pain. If I think about the past, it hurts too much. Do I want to think about that shit? My dad slowly dying of cancer? My mom dying at fucking Heavenly, in a skiing accident? Me fighting my aunt for custody of my sister when I was eighteen and she was eight? I can't do that. So I've trained myself to feel things now and not think about the shit in the past. So my fear? My fear is that everything I care about will be taken away from me. And that's because it already was taken away when I was eighteen."

If that wasn't being vulnerable with me, I didn't know what was. His confession brought tears to my eyes.

"Oh, Ryan."

"I've just had ten years to learn how to deal with it and now? I've dealt with it. Sometimes the ways I've dealt with it haven't been great. Did I go crazy at first, fucking everything in sight? Yes. Have I overindulged on all sorts of things? Yes. I cut loose, but then I got it together, for my little sister. I have to watch it. Too much pleasure means that you get fat and drunk and high and never do anything. So I surf. It clears my head." He let out a breath and smiled, a wry smile, and lowered his voice. "We can talk about all of that more. If you want. I don't particularly want to. But I'll tell you anything, beautiful. Anything." He leaned over and kissed me, a soft, wet, sweet kiss. "Are we done here, and can I take you back to bed, or is there anything else on your shit list from last night?"

Those women had planted a seed in my soul so dark and deep that I hoped that I could weed it out, because if I allowed it to grow, it could destroy this relationship—whether this was a relationship with a small "r" or a big "R."

I sighed. Then I went for it.

"Yeah, well, they were saying that you were a cheater and you used the same 'sensualist' line on them that you used on me. It made me feel like I had been had."

"The fuck?" he exploded. "Those fucking bitches. They're such haters. I can't believe they would say those things. *Fuck.*

"Listen. I've never seriously dated any of them. I've never been exclusive with any of them. I have gone to public events with a lot of them, and yeah, I've fucked a few of them, but there was nothing more. I've never been exclusive with anyone, ever. I would never cheat on anyone if I was exclusive."

"Are you exclusive with me?" I asked in a timid voice.

"Fuck, yeah," he said emphatically. "If I had found you earlier, I would've been exclusive with you earlier. I keep telling you, because it's true: you're the only one I have ever wanted. In. My. Entire. Life. I have compared every other woman who I have ever been with to you. Since high school. And even though I built you up in my mind, the real you is better. Much fucking better."

Whoa.

Hold up.

"I'm yours and you're mine."

"Are you asking me or telling me?"

He laughed. And then he asked me, in that panty-dropping, husky, sexy, low voice: "Amelia, will you go out with me exclusively and be my girlfriend?"

He made my heart beat faster every time. What other answer was there to that than, "Yes?"

NINETEEN

I'm All Yours

I<small>N THE FEW WEEKS THAT</small> I've known Ryan, I've experienced many different kinds of kisses from him. He could kiss sweet, hot, sensual, demanding, light, or companionable. Fine by me; I would take them all. I didn't choose favorites here; I'm an equal-opportunity Ryan-kisser.

But my first kiss with him as "official" boyfriend-and-girlfriend? He took the opportunity to introduce me to a new kind of kiss that, had I imagined it before, I would've told you that it only existed in an alternate universe.

It didn't.

He got out of his chair on the terrace, and kneeled between my thighs, his bare, fuck me, bare, muscled, warm chest, right there for me, like some sort of boy banquet, and his blue, flowered swim trunks dropped below his hip bones. My thighs parted biblically to let him in. Wrapping his arms low around my waist, he pulled me forward by my hips, and he pressed his hardening oh-boy into my hoo-ha. And he stayed there, his arms around me, on his knees before me, looking up at me. I responded by pulling him even closer, my arms around his neck, my hands grazing the nape of his neck, loving the way his hair curled.

Yeah, this was a fucking *awesome* place to be, in his arms on a sunny morning.

But he made it even better by observing me for a moment. A beat. Just looking at me, accepting me, letting me be there with him, in his arms. I looked back at him, and then started reviewing his boyish freckles, his cheekbones, and his handsome jaw. As I gazed at his mouth, he leaned in and brushed his full lips against mine, first to the right, then to the left, and then pressed in the middle, a full-lipped kiss, giving me him, all of him.

I parted my lips, and his tongue found mine, joining together, enjoying being with each other, enjoying kissing, enjoying the connection of our warm, moist mouths and our bodies. He leaned into me, I leaned into him. We were equal participants in an utterly active kiss. We took our time, licking the inside of each other's mouths, gently probing, then building the kiss so it was stronger and stronger. With this kiss, I gave him myself, and he gave me himself, and it was beautiful.

He left my mouth, and started leaving open, wet kisses down my chin, straight down my neck, on the most vulnerable part of my throat, in front, while I kissed his nose, his forehead, the top of his head, as he made his way down. Then he said authoritatively, lips against my neck, "Come to bed."

I nodded. He wrapped my legs around his waist, and easily got to his feet, me with all four limbs wrapped around him, like a full-frontal baby monkey.

"Do you work out?" I queried, as he walked me across the enormous full-windowed, sunny room to his big, comfy bed, his face buried in my neck.

"Sometimes. If I can't get a session in."

"Session?" I asked.

"Surfing session," he said, with a low chuckle. "This kind of session doesn't count as exercise. It counts as pleasure."

He planted me in the bed, and leaned over to take off my t-shirt.

But I had a different idea. I pushed him back with my hand.

"Wait, Ryan."

He regarded me, confused.

"Can I try something?"

"What?" he asked interestedly, his head cocked, his eyebrows coming together.

I heard the waves crash outside.

I started, hesitantly, "Ryan, you're always Mr. In-Charge in the bedroom, but you know, I haven't really had a chance to explore your body—"

"I'm all yours," he interrupted.

I'm all yours.

He was all mine.

All mine.

Mine.

"I want to return the favor of learning your body really, really well."

"Do your worst," he said hoarsely. "Where do you want me?"

Now, I hadn't really thought this through. As bossy as he normally was, he showed me repeatedly that deep down he was a giver. He didn't take anything that wasn't his to take. But now that he was letting me have my way with him, whatever I wanted, there was simply too much territory to choose from. I mean, with these options, where do you begin to explore? I couldn't decide where to start.

Okay, actually I could.

He stood by the bed, so I decided that I wanted him to stay there. I loved how he towered over me. I got up off of the bed, and reached for the hem of my surfer-shirt sleepwear, slowly pulling it over my head. Now I was wearing nothing but my satin, sage green panties and a smile. It was my turn to prowl. I lingered, circling him, not touching him, just looking him up and down. He was so tall, so muscular, so fine.

I decided to start my investigation at his back. He had these two attractive indentations, like dimples, in his lower back above his ass. Since he normally didn't have his back to me, I didn't often get to inspect them, and I decided that they needed a closer review. With my knuckle, I grazed one, then the other, and watched as his muscles jumped below his skin. Then I used my knuckle to gently trail up his spine, getting to know each vertebrae of his perfect back. I stopped my hand at the nape of his neck, and went up on my tiptoes. Sticking out my tongue like a point, I licked and sucked my way back down his backbone, while I feathered my hands out over his shoulder muscles, wings, and then down his lean sides to his waist. As I did this, I could feel him straining to stay still, straining to breathe, straining to keep his hands at his side, his body in check.

This turned me on.

Yeah. Understatement.

Watching this big handsome guy keep it in check for me to have my way with him made my panties fucking soaked.

As I've mentioned, I'm a particular fan of the inguinal ligaments that covered his hips and dipped into each side below his waist, leading to the V in the front. Now, they deserved attention. I lightly traced my fingers over his cut muscle, then reached barely inside the waistband of his low-slung board shorts, one finger on each side of his, and brought my hands together to the middle of his back, feeling the warmth of his body.

Playing with him, I lazily kept one hand just barely inside his waistband, as I moved his arm so that I could duck under it without losing the connection with his shorts, while I moved to his front. I was greeted with his erection meeting my fingers, just the tip of it. So I touched it, just a graze, and went on by, stopping at the fastening on his shorts.

My fingers traced the soft hair of his happy trail, widening my fingers out, going up, headed to his belly button.

I was sure that he thought that I was going the wrong direction.

I inserted my tongue in his navel, while following what I could see of his V with my fingers, and he groaned loudly.

Then I traced my tongue up from his belly button, paying particular attention to his washboard waist, each part of his six-pack gently defined. His breath came in ragged gasps. My hands next went to his hips, then moved inward, feeling every nook and cranny of his abdominal muscles. I made my way slowly up his torso, stopping at one nipple to suck it, and lick it, until it was hard. Then my mouth made its way to the other one, repeating the sucking, the licking, until it, too, was hard. He moaned and let out a breath, seemingly unable to keep his hands still. I reached up on my tippy toes and sucked on his neck, my hands reaching up to the top of his shoulders. My fingertips then trailed down his arms, stopping to really feel his biceps, and his sculpted forearms. And I clasped his hands, taking a step back, holding both of his hands in mine, and surveying him.

"What?" he asked, choking it out.

"You are a fine specimen of a man, Ryan Fielding."

He gave me a lopsided grin. "You're killing me, here, but it's a pretty fucking great death. Are you going to kill me now?"

"Nope. More torture first."

I let go of his hands and reached for the fastening of his shorts, undoing it, and easing them down his body, feeling his hard ass as I let it down, bending my body. His erection sprung free right by my lips.

So.

His cock.

It was beautiful, yes. It was enticing, yes. It had given me a bunch of orgasms, yes.

But I still did not feel like I knew it. Its ways were still a mystery to me.

"Ryan?"

"Yeah."

"I need to work up the nerve to, uh, you know, kiss you here."

"It's okay."

"I've never done it before."

"It's okay," he repeated. "I'll wait until you're ready. I'm not going to force you to do anything."

"I want to, I want to try, uh, well, but I'm scared."

"Amelia?"

"Yeah."

"You really are killing me now."

"Sorry. I don't mean to kill the moment. I'm trying to get over my neuroses. Are you disappointed?"

"Truth?"

"Yeah."

"I'm a guy. I always want a blow job. But I'm not going to push it on you."

"Can I try this?" I reached out and tentatively touched his cock. He shuddered and nodded, biting his lower lip.

"Fuck yeah, baby."

Again, I could hear the waves crashing outside, in and out of my consciousness.

Now, yes, I've touched a penis before. But before, it felt almost like an obligation. Something that I *had* to do. But with Ryan, it's something sensual that I *wanted* to do for him. It would give him pleasure, and for all the pleasure he gave me, I really wanted to return the favor. It also helped that his cock was astonishingly attractive. I mean, it belonged in a museum or something.

But I just couldn't do a blow job. Not yet. I didn't know why. I just … couldn't.

A hand job, though …

I touched his cock and gently stroked it up and down, first with my fingertips, noticing the vein on the underside, noticing the lip of it against the cock head, then clasping it in my hand. It was so long, I had no idea how I would ever get that thing in my mouth, if I ever decided to take him that way. But that was for another day.

He moaned again.

Moving on, I bravely took my other hand and felt his balls, gently touching them, caressing them, and this made him hiss. Then I stroked his cock, up and down, up and down, with one hand, with increasing pressure and increasing speed, and he looked down at me, eyes blazing, and growled, "Enough." He picked me up by my armpits, and threw me on the bed.

Guess he was done with me being in charge.

He tore off my panties, and fell over my body, propping himself up on his elbows, eyes on mine.

"Your turn."

He kissed my lips hard, so hard, then went down my body with his mouth, taking one nipple in his mouth and tweaking it hard, so hard that I gasped, but the bite felt so good. And then he took the other one in his mouth, and tweaked it so that the hard suck felt oh so good and then he bit his way down my side, little nibbles that tickled, until he reached my hips. While leaning on one side of me, he took his other hand and ran it up my inner thigh to the, uh, promised land, where he found me soaking wet.

Yeah.

This whole foreplay thing seemed to work.

He figured this out, too, saying, "Fuck me, you're so wet." I wasn't going to fault him for being obvious while we were in this position, and he started to stroke me with his big hands. He had his thumb pressing on my clit, his middle finger fucking me, reaching up, curving inside of me, so that I almost exploded from the pleasure. His fourth finger reached behind and up towards super naughty land.

This was what I needed.

He finger fucked me, not stopping, not taking a break, until I came. Hard.

The waves crashed outside, too.

He kept going, kept moving through my orgasm, extending it, letting me shudder and shake and convulse, until I quieted down.

But this was temporary.

"Got any more in you?" he asked, and I had no idea how to respond.

"Let's see," he said, and he kept at it, massaging my clit, massaging my g-spot, massaging that no-man's land (or no-woman's land) between my pussy and my no-go area and, confident bastard, I came again.

The waves crashed outside, too.

No, I was not complaining about two orgasms, in a row, in the morning, from my brand-new boyfriend.

My brain flooded with pleasure, but in this light room, with the sunlight streaming in, I went dark, a good kind of dark, focusing only on the sensation of release from so much build-up.

Ryan maneuvered over me to the bedside table and opened a drawer, pulling out a condom. He ripped it open, threw the wrapper on the floor, sheathed himself, and paused at the entrance of my pussy.

"I love the noise that you make when you slide into me," I whispered. "It's utter contentment. Pleasure. Heart stopping satisfaction. Like there is no place you'd rather be."

"That's because there isn't," he whispered back, and slid his cock into me.

No matter that we had done this before, it still felt exciting and special. He just filled me up, there is no other way of explaining it. It was such a rush of pleasure to have him fully seated in me, my slick pussy cradling his hard cock, his hard muscles pressed against my soft breasts. He looked down at me, shook his head with a smile, and buried his face in my neck. And then he started to move. He thrust into me, building me up, pleasure after pleasure, but then he stopped, and rolled over.

"You, on top," he ordered.

Now, this wasn't on any list of mine, as far as to do or not to do, but it still made me pause for some reason. Still neurotic, people. I was trying, okay? What to do?

"What's wrong?"

"I don't want to be an idiot, but I'm not totally sure what to do up here."

He smiled. "Okay, I'll guide you. First, pull your body up my cock, fuck yeah, like that, okay, now down, fuck."

I moved my body up and down on his, my knees to the side, my boobs jiggling.

"I feel like I'm all jiggly up here."

"That's the point. You're so fucking sexy riding me, titties bouncing, just let go. Let go," he commanded.

Okay. If he wanted to see titties bouncing, I think I could give that to him. I started to really move, to follow his order to let myself go, breasts bouncing, riding his cock, his arms snaking out and holding my soft, full breasts. It was starting to feel safe for me to be uninhibited with him. Sex was starting to feel safe. I looked down at him, and he was totally enjoying the ride.

This was fun. It was exciting to turn him on. It fucking turned me on. It was sexy. I started experimenting with different angles, different speeds, changing directions often, and staying in a particular place whenever I heard his breath speed up.

Then, suddenly, he flipped us over again, him on top, me on the bottom. He pulled back, grabbed my hips, pressing me to turn onto my stomach, and said in my ear, "Now is the time for true doggy style, babe, think you can handle it?"

"Yeah," I breathed, not able to do, say, or think anything else.

"Brace your hands against the headboard." He pulled my hips back, as I went on my knees and stretched out to the bed frame, and, frankly, for the first time in my life, I got into it. I gave him my ass, arching my back, and he thrust into me from behind.

Oh my fucking word.

This was awesome.

He thrust into me, first leaning back, and then he moved and bent over my back, his hand finding my clit, and informed me, "You're going to come again."

The thrusting, the stimulation, the angle, his orders. He kept at me, a pounding rhythm, until my vaginal muscles clenched and I let go, screaming like I had never screamed before. He massaged my clit through the orgasm, thrusting, prolonging it, then, when I was done, he thrust once, twice, three times, then bit my shoulder and collapsed into me, pressing both of us into the bed, breathing hard.

TWENTY

The Beach House

"**F**EEL IT, OH, YEAH, BABY, RIGHT there. Wait for it. It's coming. Now. Go."

I gripped the front of the boogie board with all my strength, white-knuckling it, as Ryan pushed me into the wave. The ocean propelled me forward, like I was caught on a conveyor belt, and the current pushed me to the shore. I caught my first wave.

That was so much fun!

This morning, after we, um, got to know each other a little bit better, Ryan made me breakfast, and I learned why he was so good at cooking. Since he was awarded custody of his little sister, Jennifer, when she was eight, and he was an adult, for the past ten years he fed her, took her to school, got her home, and made her do her homework, along with all of the other parental tasks. All of this when he was barely an adult. He was used to it. No wonder he was so at-home in the kitchen. And no wonder he seemed more mature than me most of the time. That's a lot of responsibility for a teenager. He had been through so much, and processed it, through surfing or whatever magic Ryan mojo he had going on, and now he was guiding me through it. Sun God therapy. His sister was away at college right now, but he said she was going to come home for Thanksgiving.

He cooked me fluffy scrambled eggs with gooey cheddar cheese, crisp bacon, buttered toast, and fresh fruit salad. We ate it leisurely, outside on his downstairs patio, watching the waves.

"Ryan, how did you get to be so, I don't know, accepting about your parents' deaths?"

"Truth?"

"Always."

"I wasn't. I acted out, at first. Like I told you." He shook his head "I was fucking everyone and doing a lot of unhealthy shit. I had to have therapy, too. There's no shame in it. A lot of people do it. Cleaned up my act fast, for my sister."

After breakfast, I gathered the dishes and brought them inside and felt completely out of place in his kitchen. It had appliances in it that I couldn't identify. His coffee maker could probably serve as central command for a NASA expedition to another planet. He refused to let me do the dishes and argued with me when I tried to help. In addition to being bossy, apparently he had no problem with being domestic at all times.

Once it was done, he came over to me. "I want to show you something," he said. He walked me to a library, and pulled out a yearbook. Our yearbook, the one we were both in. Sitting side by side on the floor, we paged through it, pointing, laughing, looking at the pictures and reading the inscriptions.

When we got to the page with my photo on it, it was circled. Next to it, he had written, "Her."

"I told you," he said. "It was always you. You were the one." And he leaned over and bopped me on the nose with the tip of his finger.

Later, he asked me if I wanted to learn how to surf. Since I didn't have a wetsuit, he let me borrow one of his sister's, which was a surprisingly good fit. Then we went out his back door to the beach.

The sand chilled our toes, but since it was October, the water was a little bit warmer than the usual year-round frigid Pacific Ocean temperatures, having been heated all summer long by currents from Mexico. Ryan informed me that since I was a "kook," meaning non-surfer, derogatory term, he was teasing me, he was going to teach me how to surf by first using boogie boards. He patiently helped me learn during the rest of the morning, and by the time we were done, I was regularly catching waves.

As we walked back to his home, hand in hand, boogie boards under our arms, we walked past the patio of his next door neighbor. He sat outside drinking a soda, and watching the goings-on. An older Hispanic man, wiry, tan, and leathery, with tattoos and a grey ponytail, he introduced himself to me as Rigo Montes. This, apparently, was Yoda.

The seaside community at Faria Beach was a mishmash of architecture. There were large modern homes, like Ryan's, and teeny-tiny weather-beaten shacks, all in the same stretch of beach. Yoda lived in one of these small beach cottages. Even though it was immediately adjacent to Ryan's mansion, the houses seemed like they belonged together and were friends. Yoda's home was just the thing for an old beach bum. I figured that he had lived there his entire life. I also liked that Ryan had someone looking out for him, since he had suffered such a huge loss.

Yoda smiled a huge smile at me, flashing a gold tooth, and immediately informed me, "I've known this guy here all his life. We've been neighbors all our lives. And I've never heard him talk about a woman the way he talks about you. It's nice to finally meet you, Amelia."

So, Ryan talked about me to his neighbor-guru. That made me feel warm in a way that tingled my fingers and toes. Sun God warmth. He steered me away before Yoda could say anything more. I got the idea that Yoda told it like it was, and wasn't afraid of potentially embarrassing anyone. We walked back into Ryan's home.

"Wanna get cleaned up?"

"I don't have any clean clothes here," I answered.

"You don't need clothes today."

I just looked at him.

He smiled, all faux-innocent, then relented. "I'll let you borrow something of mine. Okay? C'mon, let's go take a shower." Oh boy. The two-person shower. I was looking forward to that.

The thing about a shower with Ryan, was that it involved a wet, naked Ryan, and well, some things are best kept to yourself.

Just kidding. I'll give a few hints.

I gave him shit about having a double-headed shower in California, with all of our emergency drought restrictions and long-standing history of water law issues, due to our desert and quasi-desert environment. I included a detailed discussion of the controversy surrounding engineer William Mulholland's role in the 1928 St. Francis dam disaster, the legal wars over the Owens Valley water project, and the ecological damage of the Colorado River Storage Project.

See, I read more than just Harry Potter.

I asked him if he was listening, and he said, "Not in the slightest, keep talking though," because as I gave him this information, I sucked on his neck and stroked his cock until he came, moaning loudly, all over the window, which had steamed up.

I ran my finger through his cum and made a very pretty pattern.

In turn, after his body relaxed, and his eyes focused, he turned his attention to me, and gave me a detailed explanation as to exactly why his home was ultra-eco-friendly, including a dissertation on the finer points of some fancy system for his shower that I didn't pay any attention to. He told me this while lapping at my nipples, and fingering my pussy, so if there was going to be a test on it later, I didn't think I'd pass. I didn't care.

Wet, naked Ryan.

Sigh.

Afterward, in Ryan's colossal walk-in-closet, he handed me a wifebeater tank and a pair of boxers to wear.

No, it wasn't obvious that he wanted to see my breasts or anything. Perv.

I humored him and put them on without a bra. I only had my strapless one from the dinner anyway. Late October in California was plenty warm enough, and if I got cold, I'd borrow a sweatshirt. He put on a pair of boxers himself, and then put on cut off sweatpants and a plain black t-shirt that was very tight, and potentially dangerous for my blood pressure. While I dressed, I fingered the flap in the boxer shorts and commented, "I don't have, you know, boy parts to put here."

He laughed and came over behind me, stroking down my bare arms. "Do we need an intervention on what you call my dick?"

"Probably."

"Say it."

"Dick. You're a dick."

He chuckled. "No. What do you call male genitalia?"

"Um, cock?"

"What else?"

"Member. Shaft. Willy. Pecker. Peter. Johnson. Schlong."

"Can you even say the word 'penis'?"

"Penis." I forced it out.

"You cringed. Why do you avoid the word?" He continued to stroke my arms up and down, giving me major goosebumps.

This was actually a good question. If I wasn't comfortable talking about his, uh, schlong, I wasn't comfortable getting up close and personal with it.

I just looked at him and said quietly, "I'm trying, Ryan."

He wrapped me up in his arms, one on my belly, one around my shoulders, and kissed the back of my hair, inhaling deeply. "You totally are." He paused. Then, "Have we broken all your rules yet?"

"Nope."

"Good. More to look forward to."

"Wait, bastard, you know full well we haven't broken all of my Rules."

"Yeah. I was just testing you. It's my mission in life to make sure that we do." This warmed me in some very special places. "So I have a question for you. You're a professional, intelligent woman. You've been on your own and taken care of yourself. And you're obviously a feminist. Do you think you can be a feminist if you suck a guy's cock? If you suck mine?"

I looked at him, startled. "That's actually a good question."

"Can you answer it?"

"I don't know. I've never thought about it. But that might be part of my problem. My Rules started as a way of me protecting myself. I mean, I'm a badass." He rubbed his nose back and forth in my hair. "I have this thing against demeaning myself."

"So sucking cock is demeaning yourself?"

"I don't know. I've never done it. But that's what I thought when I came up with my Rules."

"Are you not a feminist if you have sex with a guy?"

"I see what you're doing here. So what you're saying is that it's a logical fallacy. Being a feminist has nothing to do with having sex with a guy—at least not if you— " I almost said 'love the guy' "—do it on your own terms."

"What about if a guy takes control in the bedroom? Are you still a feminist?"

"I don't know."

"I'm just asking, Amelia. You know I respect you and I'll always respect you. We're equals. I just know what I like, and I take it if you're willing to give it to me. But this is a partnership. We both have a say here.

"And another thing. What happens in our bedroom? Or the hall, or the bathroom, or the car, or the beach, or the—"

"Yes, Ryan, I get your point."

"You don't have to tell anyone what happens between us. Be yourself. I'm not going to share. If you're a feminist here, fine. I just want you as you. But what would happen if you didn't care what other people thought when we're naked? What if you just cared about what you and I thought? And, more important, what you and I felt?"

Fucking enlightened sage again. He was right.

I turned in his arms. "So back to this idea of partnerships. We share profits and losses, eh?"

"That's right."

"Would you like me to talk to you about the Revised Uniform Partnership Act of 1994 and its successor?"

"Lecture me, counselor."

I laughed and followed him down to his living room, where we watched *Harry Potter and the Deathly Hallows, Part I*.

Naked.

That night, after dinner, he handed me some sweatpants and a sweatshirt, and we walked hand in hand, in the moonlight, picking up sea glass and sea shells, feeling the sand on our bare feet, and watching and listening to the constant waves. This was the way I normally enjoyed the beach by myself. Sharing it with Ryan, though, was really fucking special. I wasn't alone anymore.

In the middle of the night.

"Ryan?"

"Yeah." His voice was sleep-sexy and he was groggy.

I leaned into him, my lips against his shoulder. "I'm an emotional virgin. Be gentle with me."

"Always."

And he then kissed me, completely, and cuddled me to sleep.

The next morning
"Show me."

He told me that it looked like there was a swell coming in. I wanted to watch him surf, to see him in action. It was such a part of his life. I wanted to see what he did.

After making love to me, yes, it was making love, slowly and thoroughly, he put on one of his million wetsuits, and I bundled up in borrowed sweats. I walked along the beach, carrying a mug of good Ryan coffee, and watched him paddle out to the waves. There were already a lot of people out on the water, and he joined some other surfers out there.

So. My impressions of surfing.

There's an awful lot of sitting on the board with your feet dangling off to the sides, waiting for the sets of waves to come in. But once those sets came in, Ryan's surfing was a thing of beauty. I'd always thought that it's beautiful to watch anyone do anything well. This was why we liked watching the Olympics. Ordinarily I had no interest in the decathlon. But watching someone else do it well was magnificent and inspiring.

Ryan was magnificent and inspiring on his surfboard.

When it was time for a wave to come in, he would transition immediately from hanging-out-surfer-guy to active-surfer-guy by flattening himself down on his board and positioning it so that it was headed for the shore. As the wave built up, he would paddle, paddle, paddle like a crazy man with his arms, and then, all of a sudden, get up on his feet and simply ride the wave. Or at least he made it look simple. But he didn't just hang on for dear life like I imagined that I would do.

He dominated the wave. He caressed the wave. He got to know it in intricate detail. He cut back and forth, over the lip and back down again, curving his body every which way, forcing the board to do a zig-zag pattern on the water. It reminded me of the way he was with me. Totally present. Totally exploring. Totally open. But what a workout. No wonder he had such beautiful abs.

I felt like I could watch him, stay with him, and be with him forever.

TWENTY-ONE

Body Shots

Marie says that you're dating the coffee shop hottie.
True.

Hugo's text was just one of several texts and calls waiting for me once I finally checked my phone after I got back from Ryan's house Sunday afternoon. Astonishingly, I had managed to not check my cell phone all weekend long. I didn't check Twitter, I didn't check my work emails, and I didn't look at texts. I had just put it away and didn't even think to get it out. I guess I was otherwise occupied. This felt like progress.

Ryan had driven me home after I had spent the whole weekend at his house wearing his clothes. When I walked up to my front door, I wore his boxers, his shorts, his t-shirt, no bra, and some flip flops of his. No makeup. I looked ridiculous, but I didn't care. I decided to permanently co-opt his clothes. They were pretty comfy and they smelled good, like him.

After he walked me up to the door, he kissed me thoroughly, and then prowled back to his truck and took off. Then I finally checked my messages.

So this means no time for me?

I always have time for you. As. A. Friend.

Have you told him that you love him yet?

I'm certainly not going to give you that information before I give it to him.

That means you're in love. So cool, girl!

Shit.

Instantly, another message.

Hugo tells me that you're in love with Ryan. I haven't even met him yet. Why am I the last to know?

Uh, correction, Marie. Ryan would be the last to know.

Oh. I get it. Drinks. Tuesday night. Bring him.

Now everyone's bossy.

I called my mom.

"I'd like to ask Ryan to come to Thanksgiving."

"Sure, honey. If you're getting serious about him, I'd like to meet him."

Excellent. Her tone had changed. No hint of a snob this time. And, frankly, I was proud to bring him around my parents. He was a great guy, caring for me, caring for his sister, and building a business that was all his own.

It seemed that asserting myself to my mother may have shifted our relationship from me doing whatever it was that she told me to do, to, now, me doing what I really wanted to do. And actually, now that I thought about it, all of the personal growth and development that I was doing because of him, was part of getting to know myself, for real. I didn't have to do what I thought my mom wanted me to do. The individualization that my therapist talked about was happening; I was starting to become a true adult.

First thing Monday morning, Jake walked into my office.

"I'd like your help on the Chodos matter. We were just served with the complaint and I think we need to file a demurrer. I know you don't like to bring those, but I think there's a chance that we could get the punitive damages knocked out altogether."

Yeah. Back at work again after my weekend of sex, surfing, and the Sun God. Back in the suit after wearing essentially nothing for most of the weekend.

"Is it venued here in Santa Barbara?"

"No, they filed in Ventura."

Bonus. More time at Southwinds. "I'd love to help, Jake. I'll get the file from Neveah and get started."

I remembered to text Ryan.

Marie ordered you to come out with us Tuesday night for drinks, but I figured I'd be polite and ask you instead. Can you come?

Sure.

Beware. She'll probably be ... Marie.

I can handle it, Movie Star.

I squeezed in a therapist appointment during my lunch break on Monday.

"So I'm confused about trusting Ryan. He's never done anything to make me not trust him. But I still wonder, after what those women said. Am I making a mistake?"

"Who is to know?" asked my therapist. "Mistakes happen. How do you feel when you're with him?"

"I feel cherished," I said in a small voice.

"Then that is what you need to trust. You're the lawyer. Look at the evidence. The evidence suggests that he is capable of caring, and shows it. He seems to have made a lot of headway with you, with ease. Why don't you try trusting that?"

"Because I have been hiding behind sarcasm and fear all of my life. And I've come to the point where I'm ready to just say, 'fuck it. This is me. If you don't like me, that's your problem. But I am not going to hide anymore.'"

Christian Gray smiled. "I think you're experiencing a real breakthrough, Amelia."

Tuesday night, Ryan and I walked into the watering hole on State Street, holding hands, and were greeted by a screaming, blue-haired Marie sitting in a booth, waving her arms like she was at a concert, next to a scared, but decent-looking guy, with a rather sexy man-bun.

"Here it comes," I muttered.

Ryan gave my hand a squeeze.

We walked over, and I slid in across from Marie, Ryan following. "Hey," I breathed.

Marie looked Ryan up and down and said, "He'll do." And then she declared that we were doing tequila body shots.

"Nuh-uh. No way, sister. This is a school night," I said.

"Just one each, then."

I rolled my eyes. I'd never actually done this. Marie immediately called over the waitress, and ordered four tequila shots with lime.

"Ryan, meet Marie," I said with eyebrows raised, trying not to laugh.

"Pleasure," he said, shaking her hand.

"And this is Jeremy," she said, referring to Man-Bun. We shook hands and then he shook hands with Ryan. Poor Man-Bun looked nervous. "I met him at Tri-County Produce. Okay, so I read this joke on the internet, are you ready?"

"No," I said.

Marie ignored me. "A hot blonde walks into a bar and ordered a Double Entendre. The bartender gave it to her."

I groaned and Ryan laughed. Man-Bun looked like he was in over his head and he knew it. The tequila arrived. "Have you ever done this?" Marie asked.

Shaking my head, I said, "You're the only one weird enough to do this."

"Not true. Okay, first, you lick," and she reached over to Man-Bun, and licked his neck, near his shoulder.

Oh dear. I could see where this was going. Man-Bun was in danger of hitting the table from the bottom, via an erection caused by busty Marie licking his shoulder. She was such an exhibitionist.

"Next, salt." And she shook some salt on his neck, with vigor. She could have melted a snowy street with that much salt. Too bad we were in California.

"Then the shot and lime." She licked the salt off of Man-Bun's neck, taking an indecent amount of time to do so, downed the shot of tequila, and then sucked on her lime wedge, smirking. "Simple. Your turn."

"Marie!"

"Not getting out of this one, sister."

I let out a breath. Fine. This is what happened when you were best friends with a crazy party girl. I leaned over to Ryan, pulled his shirt collar over to the side, and then sucked and licked on the part where his neck met his shoulder. He let out a very quiet groan. Then I picked up the salt shaker and poured salt on my dear Sun God. I turned back and looked at her. "Marie, this is ridiculous."

"Quiet. Just do it."

I leaned over once again and licked and sucked the salt off of Ryan's neck, tasting him, tasting his manflesh, smelling his good, sexy smell, and I may have decided to hang out there, ignoring the next step in the process.

"Amelia," warned Marie.

Stopping for a second, I looked over at her, smiled my "who me?" smile, and downed the shot, reaching for the lime. The tequila actually didn't taste all that bad—I'm not much of a shot drinker—and the alcohol warmed me up immediately. I looked over at Man-Bun, who still looked like he was trying to not have an erection. Marie grinned and clapped her hands. My crazy, crazy best friend.

"Now it's your turn, Jeremy," she said to Man-Bun, and held out her neck. He licked her neck, once. Then salted it, once. Then licked it again, once. Then did the shot and sucked the lime.

Bor-ring.

I didn't think Marie was going to ask him out again.

"Now it's your turn, big guy," she said to Ryan.

I expelled the air I was holding in my lungs.

Ryan, being Ryan, Mr. Pleasure, took his time with each

movement. He completely ignored Marie and Man-Bun, looked me in the eyes, and winked. Then he reached over, slowly, languidly, and took his index finger and used it to peel my shirt down my shoulder. He smiled, again, and slowly bent towards me, licking my shoulder. He licked it like it was his job to lick my shoulder.

I might have let out a not so soft groan.

Reaching for the salt shaker, Ryan held it aloft over my shoulder, and then, with a flick, let some salt fall on me. Then he reached in for the kill, basically taking me on the bench next to him.

I could hear Marie breathe out, "Oh," pause, "my God."

With a final suck, Ryan pulled back, downed the shot quickly, and sucked on the lime. Then he sat back in the booth.

We all looked at each other.

"I think I need a cold shower," said Man-Bun.

Several drinks later, I stumbled to the bathroom at the back of the bar, way too drunk for a Tuesday night. My designated driver, Ryan, had switched to water, thank goodness.

Once I came out of the bathroom, the room seemed to tilt. I righted myself, and started to head back to our booth, when I was stopped by a blonde woman. Botox, tight clothes, the whole Barbie vibe.

"Are you with Ryan Fielding?"

I looked at her blankly, too drunk to properly respond.

"You should be careful. He'll try and do anything to get you into bed, and then he'll leave you. Just be careful."

Some of the alcohol wore off quickly. "Who are you, some bitch he scorned? Get a clue. He just wasn't into you. There's no need to take it out on someone else. I don't need your fucking warning." Her mouth dropped open and she went to speak, but I continued, drunkenly holding up my index finger, "Not another word."

And then I tottered down the hall to my sexy Sun God and crazy best friend, who were waiting to go home.

TWENTY-TWO

Giving

So have you given him a blow job?

Marie! No.

Why not? It's rule number what? Aren't you breaking them all these days?

Rule 4. And no, I'm not. I have standards.

You are so weird.

Am not.

Are too.

Are we six years old?

Fuck no. We're talking about blow jobs on your surfer hottie.

Or, we're talking about NOT doing blow jobs on my surfer hottie.

Have you ever done one? Ever?

Amelia?

Hel-lo?

No.

Then, girl, I love you, but what do you know?

At this point, I have no idea.

Look, do whatever you want. But he'll thank you for it. You may surprise yourself and get something out of it too.

Don't you think it is, I don't know, demeaning? Being on your knees? Sucking some guy's Iditarod?

Fuck, you're messed up. No. Not with the right guy. It's a gift for him and for you. Find out what it means to really turn someone else on.

And not sure an Alaskan husky race reference is appropriate in this circumstance. Can't you just say "rod"?

[Muttering] I'll think about it.

Are you agreeing to think about giving poor, suffering, surfer hottie Ryan a blow job? Or thinking about properly referring to a guy's junk through socially-established euphemisms?

Both.

Hmm. A gift for Ryan.

Friday evening, I opened the door of my little home to let Ryan in after a long week of work. Before I could help myself, I tackled him. Mouth on his. Tongue in his mouth. Hands in his hair. Body pressed up to him.

He tackled me back, hands on my ass, leaning down and kissing me like we hadn't seen each other in a week.

Well, we hadn't. Or at least not since Tuesday.

I broke apart and he growled, low in his throat, and I grabbed his hand and pulled him into my hallway. He followed me down the hallway toward my bedroom. I didn't touch him, didn't look at him. Instead I just pulled my shirt off over my head. I could tell by the soft "swoosh" noise that he had followed suit. Then my pants were off and, again, I could tell, so were his. We left a trail of clothes in the hallway, leading up to the bedroom. Talk about zero to undressed in ten seconds. I still was wearing my underwear, and he was in his boxers, but I knew that wouldn't last long.

Looking back and leaning up to kiss him, I saw his erect cock tenting his boxers, and it was just the sexiest thing.

I kissed him lightly, and then exhaled, "Hi."

"Hi," he exhaled back, letting his finger trail down my nose and bop it on the end.

"Let me do something," I suggested, and pressed him into the bed.

I had thought long and hard about this.

Ha, hard. No pun intended.

Focus, Amelia.

But one of the things on my list was no oral sex. On me or on him.

Ryan had shattered the "on me" part of my Rule a while ago. And he may, or may not have continued to shatter it on a regular basis, whenever we were together. But thinking about it, on him, I finally realized that giving a guy a blow job meant more than what I had thought—at least to me. As I've said, I had thought that it was one, gross, and two, subjugating myself to a guy. Since being with him, however, I'd had a change in heart and learned a few things. If any guy deserved me going down on him, it was the Sun God. I'm no drunken whore in a club, blowing some guy for drugs. I adore the guy. But I wanted to try this my way. And I really wanted to see if I could make him crazy, in a good way.

I would admit that I was really nervous because I had never done it before—and the nerves were from wanting to make it good for him. I wanted, simply, to give him pleasure.

I looked at him on the bed, looking up at me with undisguised carnal intent. It was a good look on him. Almost as good as wet. I walked to the side of the bed and grabbed some pillows and put them under his head.

"Get comfy," I ordered.

"Okay," he breathed out.

Wearing just my panties and bra, I straddled him and kissed him, again, this time slowly and sweetly. He reached for me and I said, "Nuh-uh-uh. My turn."

He grinned and raised an eyebrow.

"I know you're all in-charge, competitive, surfer guy, but let me do something on your mellow, surfer guy side, okay. For you? For me?"

"Sure thing."

I kissed my way down from his lips to his jaw, and then to his earlobe, sucking on it gently. I could feel his cock twitch between my legs, against my panties, the muscles responsive. I sucked on his neck a little bit harder, kissed my way to his collarbone, then looked up into his eyes. His gorgeous green eyes were watching me, totally turned on, intense, and a little amused.

"What are you going to do?" he asked, teasing.

"A little of this and that," I said coyly, against his skin, making my way down his glorious muscular torso, holding onto his narrow hips. I licked each of his nipples and ran my tongue down the middle of his washboard abs to his belly button.

That was where the happy trail began. Right under the waistband of his black boxers. I stuck my nose in his navel, raised up from where

I was straddling him, and yanked his boxers down, freeing his cock, which was right below me.

I paused for a moment.

"You know I've never done this before."

I looked up at him and he looked very serious. "Yeah," he said in a throaty voice, "but I think you'll do fine."

I moved so that I could pull his boxers all the way off, and then started up his body, letting my fingers walk up his thighs. I stared, fascinated at his curly, but manscaped, pubic hair, and his impressive cock. He smelled like he had just taken a shower, all clean and Ryan-y. I ran my fingers through his hair and gently let the tips of my fingers pass over his balls. His cock twitched again, big time.

Heh heh, yeah, it was big.

Focus.

I lowered myself down so that his cock was between my breasts, and looked up at him.

"Christ," he croaked out.

I smiled and looked down, opened my mouth, and took his cock in, once, all the way down, as far as I could go, and then back out with a pop. The skin on his cock felt so soft and so satiny smooth on my lips and my tongue, even though underneath he was so hard. The tip of his cock was pointed. I decided to try swirling my tongue around it, and he groaned an "Uhmmmmmmmmm." He liked that.

I read in a magazine that guys like the part just under the head stimulated. So I used my tongue and teased it, flicking it, looking up at him, my eyes locked on his as he rested on my pillows. Next I ran my tongue around the tip some more and then decided to take him again, all the way down, into my mouth. I had to look down to do this, so I tore my gaze from his and went down with my mouth, taking as much as I could. Then I pulled my lips together, sucked, and went off the top with a pop. Then I took him again. And again. Sucking slowly, I used my hand to help. And then I looked up into his eyes again.

I realized, as I looked at him and listened to the noises that he was making, that I loved this. I loved turning him on. *It was massively turning me on to make him feel good.* And it was turning me on to give him something. Thinking this was demeaning or not feminist? I was so off-base. It had nothing to do with either of those two things.

I focused my attention on him, trying to think of ways that he would feel good. Sucking, licking, stroking, lavishing attention on him, lost in the moment, caressing him gently, teasing, giving pleasure.

And I realized, in the middle of this, that I was not just breaking a Rule. I was, yet again, opening up and he was opening up to me. In this position he was totally vulnerable. I could hurt him in this position, not the least by biting.

Of course I never would. But it was powerful to think that I could caress him and give him affection, and that this was paradoxically freeing me.

I had thought that it would be demeaning.

I was so wrong. This was the essence of love, distilled into an act: devoting yourself to another person's care. I wanted to take care of him. Poor motherless boy. Sexy, lovely man. I wanted to make him feel good. Feel amazing. Feel loved.

As I continued, I could tell that something changed. His cock swelled even bigger. I could feel a vein start to throb. I thought that he was getting close.

"Stop now, if you don't want me to come in your mouth," he

panted.

I looked up at him, and smiled around his cock. I'd decided before I'd even started, that I was staying with him the whole way through, and I was swallowing. I sucked harder, moved my hand faster, and gave him all of the attention I could.

I could feel his cum building up before it was released with a shudder, a pumping. Warm, sweet, but slightly bitter liquid, in my mouth. It tasted like sex, and I swallowed it down. It was no big deal to swallow.

But it was a huge deal to give him head. I felt quite accomplished and proud of myself.

He hauled me up him by my armpits and buried himself in my neck, me on top, him, breathing hard still, on the bottom.

"You're a liar."

I looked at him, confused.

"That was not your first time."

"Yeah, it was."

"It was the best I ever had."

I smiled. "I'm an overachiever," I said saucily. And then I muttered the truth: "Maybe that was because I really wanted to do it."

He shook his head, not believing me. Then he grabbed me, rolled me over on to my back, and said, "Now it's my turn."

And he proceeded to rock my world.

Rule #4 was broken, people.

TWENTY-THREE

Pop Rocks

B Y 9:45 ON HALLOWEEN NIGHT, the following Friday, all of the trick-or-treaters had ceased ringing my doorbell and asking for candy. Ryan had come over to help pass out candy and now gazed at me, with an undecipherable, but intent, look on his face. I went to the front door to turn off the porch light, signaling that we were closed for business.

"Amelia."

I looked at him. We had spoken on the phone or texted every day that week, and he had spent the night on Wednesday night, leaving super early in the morning to get to Southwinds the next morning. It felt like we couldn't get enough of each other, and we were spending as much time with each other as we could. But both of us were busy at work—me with my new case and him with running a business—and I was really looking forward to a quiet, long weekend with him.

Neither one of us had dressed up for Halloween, although we had felt the Halloween spirit, such that it was, by checking out the dozens of Disney princesses and ninjas who had knocked on my door. We watched *Harry Potter and the Deathly Hallows, Part II* and ate dinner in the pauses between visitors.

Every time the doorbell rang, he answered the door with me, talking with the kids, asking them about their costumes or how many more houses they were going to go to, and generally being an active participant in the process. This had the added bonus of him kissing me every time I closed the door. Score! In my neighborhood, there were a lot of families and a lot of kids, so we were up and answering the door all night long. Just so you know, that's a lot of sucking tongue with Ryan. No complaints.

But now the stream of ankle-biters had finally petered out and the doorbell had stopped ringing for about a half hour. I raised my eyebrows at him. He raised his eyebrows back and said, "I think we need to cross the rest of your rules off your list, tonight."

I burst out laughing. And then I immediately felt a pulse run through my body at the thrill of his words. Dammit, Ryan. He still had this effect on me. But of course I couldn't let him get away with a pronouncement like that, even if I was ready to at least try it.

"Oh you do, do you?" I sassed back.

"How many rules have you broken?" he countered.

I thought about it for a moment and then answered, "1, 2, 3, 4, 7, and 10, with likely 6 and 9 gone too."

He rolled his eyes. "That doesn't help, babe. Nobody but you has this crazy sex list memorized. Name the ones we've broken."

"Rule 1. We have sex in the light."

He smiled. "As it should be. Well, maybe we'll have to have a go at it in total darkness, just for contrast."

I considered this. Feeling my way around Ryan instead of seeing where I was going. Running my fingers down his ... Yeah, that would be fun. Time to consider putting a Rule back on the list for the sake of completeness. I started to tell him the next Rule, and said aloud, "Rule 2," and then remembered, oh shit, that's "no masturbation." Of course, being Ryan, he totally figured it out from the panicked look on my face, and shook his head.

"Doesn't count," he pronounced.

"What do you mean?"

"Look, I mean, it's good that you broke this ridiculous 'no masturbation' rule, but I haven't seen it. I've seen a picture of your magic wand, and I expect to see you show me how it works. I want to see you make yourself come. Put it on the list for tonight."

"Does that count as a toy?"

"Sure."

"Then that's breaking Rule 6."

He nodded his head as if to say, "Fair enough."

"Okay, shit, you're better at dirty talk than I am, Ryan, okay, Rule 3, um, doggy style, done, Rule—"

"—we're not even close to 'done' with doggy style, but point taken."

"Rule 4, no oral sex," I continued—

"—same." Fuck. Now I was thinking about doggy style and oral sex with him. Not necessarily a bad thing.

"Rule 7, no spending the night and Rule 10, uh, terminology, have been long gone."

He nodded gravely, pretending to be serious. Bastard.

"And you talk dirty sometimes, so that's Rule 9."

"I haven't even started to talk dirty to you," he replied in that low rumble.

Oh shit, what was I getting myself into?

"Ooh-kay," I said. "Well, feel free to break it whenever you like. I figured you already had. So the, uh, not broken ones," I stuttered out. He nodded.

"No submission, no loss of control, nothing demeaning."

"I can see why those are on your list," said Ryan, surprising me. "Some people don't like to be submissive. Or dominant. And I can see why you would not want to do anything demeaning. Frankly, I wouldn't really get off on making you do anything truly demeaning."

I let out a breath of air that I didn't know I was holding. But then he continued.

"Still, for completeness sake, just to get out all of this shit you've been carrying around, I think we should just go for it."

Eyes wide open, breath stopped, body frozen, hands trembling. Mine, that is. He seemed fine. Damn voodoo. It still affected me. At least I could talk.

Maybe.

"What?" I asked him.

"Look, I'm not saying I want to tie you up and fuck you .... Well. Hmm." He paused. Then he went on. "You know how I am. I say what I want us to do in the bedroom. I don't hold back. But it's hot for you to take control too. Or at least to try to," he teased.

I rolled my eyes at him.

"It might be a different kind of pleasure than I'm normally into, but I think we should try it. And take turns. Think of it as a bedroom game. And if either of us wants to stop, we stop."

Confused, I asked, "What do you mean?"

"I mean, we try it where you submit to me, and then we switch and I submit to you. You have total control over me and I have total control over you. Both of us trust each other not to hurt the other person. Right?" I nodded. "And, while like I say, I'm not really into it as a lifestyle, a little bit of play never hurt."

He continued, "This isn't real BDSM, Amelia. This is just seeing what it feels like to be bossed around in a sexual way. If you're not into it, I won't make you do it, but I'm wondering what it feels like on both sides."

"You haven't done this?"

"Not really," he answered.

So, I had thought about this before, when I had texted Ryan earlier this month about not doing anything demeaning. I still didn't want to do it. But I had also experienced the fact that what I thought something would feel like with Ryan in my imagination, often felt different in real life, and what it really felt like with him, was normally fucking awesome.

"Okay," I squeaked. "You first." Then I held my breath, again, and waited for what he would do.

A subtle change came over Ryan, as he stood up a little straighter and looked me in the eyes.

"Bedroom. Now," he said with authority.

I started to turn and walk away from him and he stopped me. "I think you forgot something."

My eyes widened and I looked at him, totally confused. What the fuck was he talking about?

"If I'm in control, you call me 'Sir.'"

This. This was the problem.

No fucking way was I ever calling him Sir. No fucking way was I ever calling anyone Sir, if I could get away with it.

No. Fucking. Way.

I shook my head. "I can't do this, Ryan."

It seemed like he was trying to hold back laughter. "So this is as far as we get, huh? We're stopping?"

"I don't know."

"Do you want to keep going? Do you want to trade places?"

I had a vision of making Ryan crawl across the room to me, naked, gorgeous ass in the air, shoulders tilting to the ground, while I wore a Dominatrix outfit and held a whip. The thing was, I didn't really want to do that to him. I didn't like feeling like he was dominant over me and I didn't really want to be dominant over him. I liked feeling like we were partners, and he was just the leader, or guide, in the bedroom, at least most of the time.

So I started talking: "In just that short period of time, I felt humiliation, relief, turned on, disgusted, and worried where my sweet Ryan was. I don't want to be humiliated. I don't want to humiliate you. I just want to feel good. I know we're just playing and I know I'm stupid and I know that I'm taking it too seriously, but I felt like I didn't like it. At all."

He pulled me into his arms. "I meant it when I said that you didn't have to do it. And I meant it when I said that I would let you do it to me."

"I don't want to do this, Ryan."

"So we're going to keep 'nothing demeaning' on your list."

"Yeah."

He smiled. I had my Ryan back. Phew.

"It's your list, babe. Keep whatever you want on it. My job is just to push you on it, but push back if you want. So, you done for the night or can we keep going?"

"So, I had an idea."

Ryan looked at me in interest.

"What kind of idea?"

"A sexual idea."

"All ears, Movie Star."

"So I've been reading a few well-written, excellent, high quality, literary books."

"Smut?" he teased.

"Yeah. Well, a couple of them had food fantasies involving whipped cream, or chocolate sauce, or peanut butter, and licking it off of each other."

"I've never heard of peanut butter."

"Sometime, Ryan, we'll try peanut butter. Well, I was thinking of—"

"Wait, you can't just say, 'Sometime, Ryan, we'll try peanut butter' and not let me enjoy that image—your pink tongue and those lips licking me. Maybe you're on your knees, your gorgeous dark hair and creamy skin sucking me off. Both of us getting all hot and sticky. Maybe a shower afterward. And then in the shower ...." He closed his eyes. "Yeah." He let out a breath of air.

"Waiting, Ryan."

He came to and opened his eyes and smiled. "Okay. Continue."

"Like I said, I was thinking of trying something a little different. The opposite of those."

"What, like, sriracha?"

I burst out laughing. "No. I think that would hurt. I was thinking more like, um, Pop Rocks. We have some left over from passing out candy."

Now it was his turn to burst out laughing.

I continued. "You know, you're the sensuous one. What do you think it would feel like, me sucking you off with Pop Rocks in my mouth? The candy popping around your cock …"

"It would either be incredible or warrant a trip to the hospital."

My shoulders slumped, discouraged.

"I'm up for it if you are."

My hand dipped in the bowl of candy and I grabbed three packets of Pop Rocks. So this would be interesting. Not bothering to move from the living room, I went over to Ryan, bopping my finger on the end of his nose, for a change. "Let's see how this feels."

Running my hands down his muscular chest, I came to the waistband of his jeans, undoing them and sliding them down his hips, slowly. Then I pushed his black boxers down so that his erection, and yeah, he was hard after all that talk, sprung free.

If I'm going to do this, I'm going to get into it. I got down on my knees before him, like he got down on his knees before me in the past, and hugged him around the waist. I could feel his warm skin and I could tell that his pulse was racing. As I'd never sucked a guy off before Ryan, I'd never done this before in this position. Gently taking his cock with my hands, I rubbed my hands along it, pumping him gently, but firmly. Then, opening my mouth, I took a tentative lick, getting a drop of precum. I loved it. Essence of my Sun God.

Ripping open the package of Pop Rocks, I opened my mouth and dumped some in, giggling. Then I quickly covered his cock all over, getting the effervescent candy popping all up and down him. I started running my tongue up and down his cock, lapping up the candy as it popped. It made him taste sugary, of course, and the sensation was overwhelming: warm, hard cock in my mouth, candy popping on my tongue. Ryan looked down at me, eyes wide, breath shortened, saying "Fuck yeah, babe." I used my hands and added more candy as they dissolved, licking him all over, getting the sweet taste of the candy everywhere.

I don't know that I've done something that free in my life. It was silly, it was raunchy, it was sensuous, and it was bold. No one was watching. So I got into it.

"I don't want to come in your mouth," he moaned. "Come on. Let me see you use your Ollivander wand, Hermione. Torture me. Let me see you pleasure yourself."

Not waiting any longer, I whipped my shirt off, undid my jeans, took off all of my clothes, and raced to my bedroom, Ryan on my heels, at first hopping with his pants down, until he got them off. As I leaned over to the bedside table to take out my vibrator, he kissed me down my spine, holding me firmly.

"Let me see it," he repeated. "Let me see you come."

I backed to the bed and lay down on it, not entirely sure what to do. Deciding that if I really got into it, it would be a show for him, I spread my legs wide, while he stood to the side of the bed. I turned on my Ollivander wand, found the right setting, and tentatively grazed it against my pussy.

And I moaned.

Wet from our discussion, from playing with him, I moved the vibrator around to wherever it felt good, as he watched.

I realized that I was letting him in, again. Never, never, never would I have let another person see me do this before. I never did it before. But now, watching how much he loved it? So fucking hot.

So yeah, my body took over after a few minutes, a few minutes where he stroked himself while he watched me, and I thought that was so fucking erotic, and when the orgasm overtook me, I threw my head back and wailed.

Then, sliding on a condom, he entered me, extending the orgasm, and making me come again, until it was his turn, and he collapsed.

Mischief fucking managed, at least for tonight.

TWENTY-FOUR

Surprises

OCTOBER TURNED INTO NOVEMBER, which in California meant that not much changed, weather-wise. It stayed sunny, for the most part, and I spent even more time at the beach house with my Sun God, for he really was my Sun God, learning to surf, and doing some other stuff. He also was frequently at my home, and we did some other stuff. And we saw each other in other places, and did some other stuff.

You can figure out what kind of stuff I'm talking about.

Okay, I'll spill.

One Wednesday, in early November, he surprised me at my office, showing up at the reception desk, holding paper bags of sandwiches for lunch. When Neveah paged me, she didn't tell me who was there, she just told me that there was a package waiting for me at the front desk. But once I walked out front, I saw my surfer standing there, with his dark jeans belted low on his lean hips, a button-down, plaid shirt over a white t-shirt, which hugged his biceps, and flip flops. Some package. His dimples made an appearance on his tanned face and his curly, light hair looked especially wild in our staid office. But a delivery of a hot, sexy man who brings me food? Yes, please.

Quietly following me down the hall to my office, not saying anything, since my co-workers were busy, he looked around, taking in the surroundings. One side of the office, the side with windows, had attorney's offices, one after another, all the way down the hall. The other side of the hall opened to cubicles for legal assistants.

Ryan's presence made me notice things that I normally took for granted. For example, I listened, and heard how the office had a quiet hum of computer keys typing, papers printing, and copy machines churning out legal documents, in addition to muffled telephone conversations. As we strode to my office, I really looked at the local photographs on the walls; over the years I had become inured to my surroundings and never really looked at them anymore, even though they were naturally beautiful. He always had this effect on me, making me feel things and experience things that I had previously numbed out or blocked.

But of course, the thing that I was most aware of was him. Ryan had this bigger-than-life presence; at least, I thought so, and I felt it. He radiated energy, which attracted me to him and made me more "me." I felt things more with him, I saw things more with him, I heard things more with him, and I felt more alive when I was with him.

More than his effect on me in a personal development sense, however, was that he still fucking turned me on every fucking time I saw him. You would think that I'd get used to it, that there would be some sort of habitualization or familiarization with his sexiness.

But no.

I thought that I'd never get used to him. It felt like he was *it*, for me. I don't think he was "my type," whatever my type was. "My type" was probably a guy in a tie. He certainly was not like any other man I had ever been with. He was so manly, but gentle, so bossy, but egalitarian. His male beauty was almost too much for me to take at times. I never thought I'd have a thing for a surfer. But here it was: the guy for me was a super sexy surfer.

What's more, I loved it when he entered the room, any room, at any time. My heart always beat faster when I saw him. He always surprised me, and I always wanted to see what he would do next. In some ways, I had always gone through life waiting for the other shoe to drop. If things were going well, I expected it to end. I expected that there was an end-date for good things happening to me. But with Ryan, it seemed like it just got better and better every time we were together. It felt like we were open with each other, like our relationship was real, and like we trusted each other.

I thought that we were the physical embodiment of the classic "opposites attract." My pale, his tan. My dark hair, his light. My soft curves, his hard muscle. But we fit each other really well. Even though we were opposites, we felt good together and balanced each other out. I imagined our relationship as the yin-yang symbol, him all hot and fiery, male passion and energy, me all feminine and, well, cool. The moon to his sun.

Oh, fuck, I've just proved that I really am a fruit and nut from California. I'll just show you to the New Age bookstore down the street and get you some organic cold-pressed green juice and a CrossFit session before you have your reading with the psychic.

Moving on.

So now he showed up in my office, a surf God in his flip flops and jeans, while I was dressed conservatively in my black pencil skirt, cream cashmere sweater, black patent leather kitten heels, and fucking pearls. Truth: I liked the pearls when I was going for the Liz Taylor lookalike thing. Okay, so I was dressed a bit like a sexy secretary. It was a good day for him to come by as a surprise.

Once we got to my office, I felt shy. Here was where I spent most of my days, and this was my sanctuary. I was showing him another part of me. I spent an awful lot of time here, so I had tried to fix it up to make it reasonably pleasant for the hours that I spent billing clients. My office was stylish, with a traditional dark wood desk and credenza, cream colored, upholstered, client chairs, and orchids that I bought regularly from an orchid grower just south of Santa Barbara. My diplomas were framed, serving as a resume on the wall. Although there were papers on my desk, and a few boxes of files on the floor, it was mostly neat.

I walked into my office and shrugged, saying, "This is me," and he looked around appreciatively. But then he closed the door behind him and launched at me with a scorching kiss. Hard, wet, and thorough. Then, as he sucked and bit along my jaw, his glorious full lips moving towards my ear, he started nibbling my ear, and murmured "I couldn't wait until the weekend."

Panties, wet.

But.

"My door doesn't lock."

We both looked at the back of my doorknob, which had no lock, but a hang tag dangling, the type that were in hotels to ask the maids to pick up the room, only this one said "Do Not Disturb, Teleconference with the Court."

Oh, that wicked Ryan grin.

He separated away from me, opened the door a fraction and slid the hang tag on the front of my door, letting it swing. Then he shut the door.

"How you doing today?" he asked, moving back towards me.

"Fine?" Where was he going with this?

"I think we can do better than 'fine,'" he whispered, and bopped my nose with his tan index finger. Then he gently pushed me toward my desk, propping my ass up so I was half-leaning on it, and got down on his knees and pushed up my skirt over my ass. Then he hooked his fingers in my panties (thank God I only wore my new pretty ones these days) and slipped down the lacy, black high-cut-showing-my-ass-cheeks panty down my legs, and off.

I noticed that he didn't take off my shoes. I wasn't gonna take them off, either.

"Spread." The tone of his voice brooked no argument. You know, I still couldn't believe that I was doing this here, in my office, essentially a public place, with co-workers all around, and an unlocked door. But I spread.

He lifted me up so that I was sitting on the desk, pushed my knees way out, farther than I had left them, and licked and laved his way up my inner thigh, heading towards the promised land in the middle.

"Fuck, I love it that you're bare," he murmured, "you are so wet you're glistening. It is, fuck, it's so—" and he didn't finish his sentence because his mouth was on my pussy, and he was therefore otherwise engaged.

As they said in some eighties movie I saw during retro night in college, *fuck me gently with a chainsaw.*

Ryan did not hold back in anything, but he especially did not hold back in thoroughly exploring my sensitive pussy. He licked, and gently sucked my clit and then ran his tongue around it, the entire length, circling both sides, hitting all of the nerve endings. Then he repeated his ministrations. Tongue on clit, then my whole pussy. Repeatedly. Over and over again. He teased with the tip of his tongue, then lapped me steadily, then teased, and was steady, until my body tensed up and built up and tensed and built, until I was about to cross that bridge into the land of the orgasm.

It seemed that the antidepressants were not an issue any more. Thank you, Dr. Google for believing in me.

No. Thank you, Sun God.

When I was about to come, my arms straight and bracing the desk, my legs spread and tensing, my eyes closed, my head thrown back, my breathing stifled by my attempt to clamp my mouth shut, he inserted one long finger, and then another into me, and then, ohmigod, started finger fucking me for real as he ate me, caressing, cajoling, and coaxing an orgasm from me.

I had to bite my lips to keep from making noise.

My entire body convulsed as I perched on my desk, Ryan's curly hair between my legs, my lips pressed together tightly, keeping a moan from escaping. My arms, holding on to the desk, shook. My breasts shook. My legs shimmied. I climaxed. I released. I came.

He stayed there, licking me, riding it out with his face and his fingers, extending it, then easing me down, as the convulsions slowed.

Then he got up, gracefully, and smiled at me, putting his forehead next to mine.

"Time for lunch?" he asked.

"Nuh-uh, buddy. Your turn. We've gone this far. Might as well christen the desk. I'll name it after you. Did you bring a condom?"

"Yeah." He pulled out his wallet, fished one out, and ripped it with his teeth. "I like the idea of you looking at your desk and thinking of me fucking you while you're working on some complicated case." Then he unbuckled his belt, lowered his pants and boxers, and let his handsome, almost fully-erect, cock be free. I rubbed his cock with my hands, bringing it to full attention, and then rubbed it against my wet pussy, lubing it up, enjoying the feel of him, the thickness, the throbbing, and the tension.

"Let me," I said, and he handed me the condom.

I rubbed his cock against my pussy, up and down, with some pressure, and now it was his turn to put a hand over his mouth to suppress a moan. Up and down, up and down, and then he looked at me, pleading, and said, "Enough, Amelia. Now." I smiled, and rolled the condom down, sheathing him. Then I spread my legs wider, and pulled him to me.

Because I was so wet, he slipped his big cock easily inside, again suppressing his satisfied moan, and he held me to him by my lower back, fucking me on my god-damned lawyer desk.

Fucked me. At work. During working hours. On my desk.

It was so god-damned quiet, just our heavy breathing, and the slaps of our skin, against the hum of the office.

Ryan sucked his index finger and then slipped it between us, rubbing my clit again.

Oh, beautiful torture. I couldn't say anything, I couldn't really move, I couldn't do anything, I couldn't think.

Finally, I was not over-analyzing sex with Ryan. *I was just doing it.* I was just feeling the connection, feeling our bodies, feeling the pleasure, feeling great. Feeling being connected to him.

Again, he built me up, and this time I came at the same time that he did, our bodies shaking together, our groans suppressed in a wild, seriously desperate, kiss.

He collapsed on me, burying his face in my neck, holding me up on my desk, his cock still inside me.

After a bit he leaned back, pulling both of us up, slipped out, divested himself of the condom and put it in the pocket of his jeans, tidied himself up, helped me on with my panties, and asked, "Now, time for lunch?"

And I burst out laughing.

A few days later, on my lunch break on Thursday, I wandered through Sephora on State Street and ended up in the NARS cosmetics aisle. Then I realized how far I had come in the few short weeks since I had known Ryan.

I had come. Ha! No need for me to buy the ORGASM blush. I looked at the other blushes and wondered how the MALIBU color would look on me instead. It seemed more appropriate with my surfer guy.

Thursday evening, I left work early, and decided to surprise Ryan at his house, the way he surprised me at my work.

Even though I was still dressed for work, with a black blazer, slim trousers, and pumps, I thought, "Fuck it," and put down the convertible top, tying my hair back. I drove along the coast from Santa Barbara to

Faria Beach, the wind wild, the sun on my skin, music playing, feeling good. I turned off Highway 101 to the turn-off and followed it along the beach, to Ryan's house,

… where I saw two people standing in his open garage door;

… where I saw a female booty in short shorts and stacked sandals on long, slim, tan legs;

… where I saw Ryan's arms wrapped around this blonde female's back, embracing her;

… where I saw him move in and press his forehead to this female's forehead;

… where my entire world died.

TWENTY-FIVE

Silly Things

B ASTARD. FUCKING BASTARD.
Words did not exist that were strong enough to express how I felt.

I realized that I had a few choices. I could go back and confront him. I could call him and yell at him.

Or I could do what I did on autopilot, and get the fuck out of there.

As I continued down the street past that fucking bastard's house, I got on the freeway at the next entrance and headed back up to my house.

My heart seized up and I didn't breathe.

My body seized up and I had no idea how I was going to drive.

My mind seized up and I couldn't think.

I couldn't deal.

Those fucking blonde bitches were right. The fucking looks I got, the fucking warning. They were all correct.

All those warnings. All those signs. I should have paid attention. I shouldn't have ignored them. I shouldn't have trusted him.

I shouldn't have trusted myself.

I should not have trusted, period.

It hurt too much to trust.

The thing was, as I drove, after a while, I realized that I was not in my deep, dark depression place. I was fucking mad. I was hurt. I was pissed. I was sad. And I was heartbroken.

But I was not numb.

And in this place of strange, unbelievable hurt, I realized that I was not shutting down. I had learned something, and I was recovering.

It fucking hurt, but I was strong, and I was getting stronger.

The feeling that I felt was not one of closing in on myself. I was not looking for a railroad track. Instead, it was hot, horribleness coursing through me, racing around, pumping through my veins.

And while it hurt, as I drove, I realized, with the training that my therapist had given me, that I was still breathing. I was still alive and I was going to make it.

I felt like I deserved a trophy for getting the fuck out of depression.

And a little part of me felt proud of myself for not collapsing into numbness and nothingness.

I was recovered. For real. At least as much as you could ever recover from a mental illness.

But I needed to get these feelings out of my body. I needed to scream, to yell, to cry, and to expel these demons.

What I needed was a pity party. I hit "call" on my phone.

"Marie, I need a pity party. How soon can you be over?"

"About an hour or two."

"Okay, here's the deal. We're having vegan cake, champagne, and we're watching *Bridget Jones's Diary*. I need medicinal Colin Firth and Hugh Grant."

"What happened with Ryan?"

"I'll thank you to never mention that low-down, no-good, dirty, rat bastard to me again. Fucking asshole."

"I'll be there in forty-five minutes, and help you frost the cake."

"Deal."

So here's the thing. I throw pity parties literally. It's a party. There's drinks. There's cake. There's a celebration. I wallow in my pity. And then I move on.

So, a half hour after I got home, the cake was in the oven, I had had a shot or three of tequila, and Marie knocked on the door. She barged in the second I opened the door, and said, "Smells good, though you smell like a bar. Give me some."

I poured her a shot of tequila, and myself another one, and we clinked shot glasses. No salt or lime this time. Too many memories with that one.

"To all of the assholes who have ever hurt us. May they go away and suffer pain like they've never felt," I toasted. I felt a twinge of guilt because Ryan had never been an asshole to me. Just a cheating bastard. Fucker.

"To the assholes," said Marie. And we downed our shots.

She handed me a CD. "Here's a present for you. Well, just put the songs on your phone and then give it back to me."

"Wild Child?"

"It's a band out of Austin. They sound like Of Monsters and Men."

"Thanks, I'll check them out."

I turned the oven timer on for the cake, pulled out the champagne and the champagne glasses, and went over to my movies to put on *Bridget Jones*.

"What happened?" asked Marie, flopping on my comfy couch. I looked at her, straight in the eye, and took a deep breath. Then I admitted the horrible thing that I'd witnessed.

"I saw Ryan with another woman."

"No!" Marie looked utterly shocked, and set down her drink.

I grabbed the remote and slunk down into the couch. "Yep. Bastard. I fell for him, hook, line, and sucker."

"Don't you mean 'sinker'?"

"Nope. I'm a sucker. And I'm drunk. And he was really the player they said he was."

Marie was loyal, but she was no fool, and she always pushed me. "Are you sure?"

"I saw him, Marie. I'm a fucking lawyer. I saw the evidence."

Her brown eyes, warm and analytical, wandered over me. "What did you see?"

"Him with a blonde in his arms in front of his house." The movie started to play, and I paused it.

Marie looked pissed. "That's fucked up. But isn't it 'innocent until proven guilty'?"

"Nope. He's no criminal. This is a civil matter. The burden of proof is 'preponderance of the evidence.'" Tequila shots ingested, and on to the champagne. I must have been getting drunk if I was starting to talk law. I never talked law with civilians if I could help it.

"Fucking men. Who needs 'em?" said Marie with a glass in her hand. I knew there was a reason why I invited her. "But are you sure about Bridget Jones's Diary? You sure you want a love triangle?"

"Good point. *Magic Mike XXL*. Best plot ever."

"What plot? I thought the plot was a road trip to a stripper convention?"

"Exactly."

I switched the movie, we settled in, feet up on the coffee table, and we watched Channing and Joe and the rest of the six-packs gyrate. At some point I took out the cake. Later, when it was still warm, we frosted it. We ate big pieces with gulps of champagne.

And we were drunk. It was a party. A pity party. I felt bad for myself, for having wrecked my life, yet again, and now I would move on.

Well, I was too drunk to move on right now. I'd think about it in the morning.

At some point we called Marie a taxi and I went to bed.

Strangely, afterward, I felt better.

I didn't call him; he didn't call me.

I didn't want to think about how I was going to have to restart my life, yet again.

Too early, Friday morning, my phone rang. It was Ryan.

Man, I was in Hangover City from too much tequila and champagne. Damn. I didn't want to talk to him, but I felt like I should pick it up. I needed to tell him what a fucking bastard he was. "What, Ryan?" I asked mulishly, and winced, since my head hurt.

An unfamiliar woman's voice, faint sounding, and wavering, asked

"Is this Amelia?" I was instantly on alert. Something was wrong. Something was very wrong.

"Yes."

"This is Jennifer Fielding, Ryan's sister. I found his cell phone and wanted to call you. He's at the hospital." I froze and stopped breathing. "He's unconscious. He had a bad accident at South Jetty while surfing early this morning, hit some rocks ..." she trailed off in a sob.

"Tell me where to come," I demanded.

"He's at Community Memorial Hospital. In the trauma unit. He's lost a lot of blood. I can't lose another one. After losing my mother and father, I can't lose my brother too," she sobbed.

Fucking hell.

I couldn't lose him either.

"Shh, shh, it's okay, I'll be there in less than an hour."

I caught a glance in the mirror. Holy hell, I looked like I had thrown a pity party last night. I piled my hair on the top of my head, slathered on some moisturizer, gulped a Gatorade, and puckered up to put on lipstick. I grabbed my purse, shoved my feet in some shoes, and headed out the door, driving like a maniac from Santa Barbara to Ventura.

I loaded the new Wild Child CD in the player to distract me from the drive.

It didn't work.

When it got to the second song, it was like I couldn't listen, but had to listen at the same time. Fuck, what a song. "Silly Things." Heartbreaking lyrics about how a relationship started around a coffee pot until silly things got in the way.

No time to process.

I slid into the parking lot, barely remembering to lock my car doors, and ran into the hospital.

"Ryan Fielding," I panted to the information desk.

"Are you family?"

"He's my boyfriend." Or was, at least.

The information desk checked his records on the computer. "He's in surgery on the fourth floor. You can wait for him in the waiting room up there, although I don't know if you will be able to see him."

I didn't care. I would find a way to see him. I ran-walked past the gift shop to the elevators. Once the elevator door opened, the car lumbered up. Could they make slower elevators?

It was not like getting there faster was going to make him better but still, I had to be there. I didn't have time to sort out all my feelings. I was just reacting.

I'd never met his sister, never seen a picture of her, so I was not sure where to look for her.

The elevator opened and I walked into the waiting room.

She was there.

A beautiful blonde with long legs and long hair. Wearing short shorts and stacked sandals.

The blonde who was hugging Ryan.

She was crying and holding his phone.

His phone.

His green eyes.

His sister.

Shit.

I'd made a mistake. A fucking mistake that belonged in a two-bit romance novel. I had jumped to conclusions, yet again, because I couldn't trust the good that was around me.

We all did this. Why couldn't we be happy with what we are given? Why do we have to assume that something needs to be wrong? Why can't we just live and be naturally happy? Why do we need to constantly look over our shoulders, waiting for some bad thing to happen? Why do we assume that it's going to happen? Why do we assume that people are going to let us down?

What I had learned with Ryan was that it all boiled down to trust, opening yourself up, and vulnerability. I had trusted Ryan, opened myself up to him, and been vulnerable with him. And I'd never felt better in my life. I had never felt more *alive* in my life.

Whatever psychological need I had to make him a bad guy could stop right now. I didn't need to go looking for something wrong with him, which is exactly what I had done.

I turned to his sister.

"Jennifer?" I asked.

She looked up at me, the same eyes as her brother, but put on a different, softer, female face. "Amelia. Ryan has told me so much about you." Her pretty lip trembled.

"Shh, shh, it's okay," I soothed her, although I knew that I was the one who was going to need to be soothed.

What an asshole I had been.

Again.

I assumed that Ryan was a surf bum. I assumed that he was a coffee shop manager. I assumed that he was insincere. I assumed that he cheated on me.

I had assumed the worst of the best guy that I'd ever known. I was glad that this most recent assumption only lasted a night. And I was glad that he wouldn't ever know, unless I told him.

I wasn't going to live my life in fear of how he was going to hurt me. I had been hurt before and I had survived and if it happened again, I would fucking survive, again. But I wasn't gonna go looking for bad shit about the most marvelous man I'd ever met. The one who had crushed on me for a decade. I was just going to trust that it would be okay. Starting here, today, in the hospital.

He wasn't any of those bad things that I had thought or that had been told to me. He was just Ryan, the man that I love.

And now he was hurt.

Fuck.

TWENTY-SIX

Heartbeat

Hours later

"A MELIA," RYAN RASPED AS HE opened his groggy green eyes.

I had spent hours at the hospital with Jennifer, waiting for news about his condition. I called into work to beg off due to an emergency, then checked my messages so many times that my phone died. I had forgotten the phone charger, and ended up staring at the posters on the walls, flipping through magazines, and jumping with a start anytime anyone opened the door. I was wired from caffeine from too much coffee. Bad coffee, not like his amazeballs coffee. Ugh.

My Sun God touched every part of my life.

During the hours that we waited, Jennifer and I talked, not awkwardly, but there were long periods of silence since we were both nervously waiting for news. I found out that she had come home a week early from college because she had arranged her classes so that she had a long break. She told me that she wanted to teach kindergarten and was working on getting her teaching credential. She had stayed up late last night talking with Ryan, and they had lost track of the time. Then he went out surfing this morning, early, at the south jetty of the Ventura Harbor, hoping to get in a session before work at Southwinds.

I knew where the harbor was, an area with shops and restaurants on one side, but several rocky jetties on the other side to protect the boats moored in the harbor. Apparently the area had amazing surf, but it was very dangerous. Even if you knew the area well, you could still get hurt. Jennifer told me that the area is really shallow and has hollow waves, which made it attractive to surfers, but you could get slammed on the shore. A really famous surfer got his neck broken there recently.

I didn't want to think about that.

After a long, long time, we were told that Ryan was out of surgery and they were moving him to another room.

Then we waited a long, long time and we were told that we could visit him.

We went into the room together, instinctively holding hands. Ryan was lying in a bed, asleep, with machines beeping. There were wires and an IV and medical things around him. I had no idea what most of it was. But I realized that one of the machines broadcast the steady beat of his heart, and this soothed me.

It had been my experience in hospitals that people normally looked smaller, diminished, when they were lying in a hospital bed, surrounded by medical equipment. Not Ryan. He was so tall and muscular, with his broad chest and defined biceps that he took up the whole bed, and he looked beautiful. And while he was asleep and was bandaged up, he still looked strong.

He had a bandage on his temple, some cuts and bruising on his face, his arm in a cast, cuts on his other arm and hands, and apparently some broken ribs that I couldn't see under the blanket. While he was pretty beat up, and was unconscious when they took him to the hospital, the doctor told us that the prognosis was good.

Hope.

I needed something to hold on to.

I decided to hold on to his hand. I waited for him by his bed, gently stroking his hand, and looking at his handsome sleeping face. Jennifer stayed with me the whole time. It was heartbreaking to realize that she had no one else to call for him, except me, and perhaps, Yoda. They had no parents. And Ryan had told me that he was estranged from his aunt after battling her for custody of his sister. I didn't know if there were any other family members. After a while, when she was falling asleep in the chair, I sent her home and told her that I would stay there until she came back.

I didn't know how much later it was when he finally opened his eyes. While I normally lost any sense of time with him, this was something entirely different. It was like I was willing him to get better, willing him to recover, willing him to be my Ryan again.

Because he was my Ryan. My idiocy over silly things and wrongful conclusions, well, I hoped it was a thing of the past. I was not going to be so unrealistic as to say that I would never again jump to stupid conclusions about my awesome guy, but I was going to try like hell for it to be never again.

I trusted him. He was it for me. And I loved him.

And when he opened his eyes, I wanted to tell him.

Fuck it. I wasn't going to wait any more and if the feeling wasn't reciprocated, oh well. I was going to take the risk. Life was too short and I had shut myself down, kept myself from risking, from feeling, for too long. Maybe I had a good reason for doing so, but I needed to move forward. He mattered to me and I was going to tell him; I was not going to keep anything from him. If I got hurt in the process, I knew that I would survive. I was strong.

"Ryan," I whispered, as he looked around the hospital room.

"I guess I ate it big time, huh?" he asked with a small smile. Then he asked me what happened and I told him what I knew. He lifted his finger and stroked the back of my hand.

After a while, he closed his eyes and dozed, and I dozed with him, sitting in a chair by the bed, my forehead by his hip, holding his hands, as the machine beeped, singing his heartbeat to me.

I woke up later and looked at my Ryan, vibrant eyes open, propped up in bed, looking at me.

"Movie Star, you need to go home and take care of yourself."

I felt groggy and gross, wearing the same clothes that I had thrown on who knows how many hours ago. I had basically no makeup and my hair was thrashed. I'm sure I looked like a total a mess. I didn't care. I was with him.

"I don't want to leave you."

"You're not leaving me," he said with a smile. "You're just going to get some sleep and a shower."

"Well, maybe in a little bit. How are you feeling?"

"I don't know that I've felt much worse," he admitted. "I have a headache, but I think the drugs are keeping me from feeling too much pain right now."

"What would make you feel better?"

"Honestly, some water. All these ice chips are getting to me."

I went and got him some contraband water, medical rules be damned, and he drank it gratefully.

Taking a deep breath, I started, "There's something I need to tell you."

"I'm listening."

"I'm an idiot. I was really mad at you and you didn't do anything wrong. I wanted to surprise you at your house and I drove by and I saw you hugging your sister and I thought that she was, fuck, was … ."

His eyes widened and he dipped his forehead down to look at me.

"Fuck, I'm sorry, that I ever doubted you. I jumped to conclusions about you, yet again. You've never done anything to me except be honest with me. You've been honest with me about your feelings, about what you're thinking, about what you want to do. I'm the fucked up one and you've helped me to be less fucked up." And then I just went for it. "I like myself when I'm with you. I lose myself in you but I also find myself in you. You're the best friend I ever had and the best lover I ever dreamed of. I love you."

He tensed his hand on my hand and looked at me. My heart beat so fast I thought it would outpace the machine that he was hooked up to.

"You've been the only one for me since I saw you on the first day of school all those years ago, and I've carried you in my heart since then. But I didn't know you then. And now that I know you, I *know* I love you." He continued in a whisper, "You're the only person, besides members of my family, who I have ever loved and the only one I ever will love."

I leaned over and kissed him very softly on his lips, avoiding his cuts. Then I kissed his eyelids, very soft butterfly kisses. Then I brushed my lips over his forehead and inhaled his soft hair.

He smiled at me and said, "Go home, get some rest, get a shower, and then come back."

"Are you asking me or telling me?"

He smiled. "A little bit of both."

RYAN RETURNED HOME FROM the hospital a few days later, with his arm in a cast and his beautiful torso bandaged up. He also had some stitches on his temple that were covered in a bandage.

I took a leave of absence from work to take care of him and I found that I loved taking care of him. While he did not like to be lying down—he was normally all energy—he seemed to be channeling this energy into healing rather than anything else. So he got better at a faster rate than the timeline that the doctor told him that he could expect.

During this time, I found that I was healing as well.

I would never really recover completely from depression. There were too many scars, too much pain. There was always going to be a part of me that reacted to uncomfortable events in my life by shutting down, by numbing myself out, by avoiding my feelings.

But those times were starting to come less and less and I called that fact, "recovery." I also consciously tried feeling all of my feelings, both the pleasurable and the painful, and I survived. But I felt like more than a bare survivor; I felt like I was starting to thrive.

I found that I was not needing to see my therapist as much. I still saw her, but not multiple times a week as I did before I met Ryan. I still took antidepressants, but I could take a lower dose. My mood stayed mostly stable.

I also found that I was only rarely having nightmares about hospitals anymore—not about my time in the hospital, my time in the mental hospital, or Ryan's time in the hospital. I was generally having sweet dreams (and they normally featured him naked). After he got healthy, he was perfectly willing to reenact any part of them that I remembered.

It was many weeks before I could launch myself at him with any vigor.

But those parts came back too.

Ryan missed Thanksgiving because of the hospital, but he was well enough to make a big deal about Christmas. I learned that he usually went all-out for his sister on holidays, trying to make it a special day for her, given the absence of any other family in their lives. He bought two Christmas trees, put up lights everywhere so that it looked like a fairy had exploded, made sure we all went to Candy Cane Lane to look at the over-the-top Christmas lights, and even took us to a professional performance of the Nutcracker in Los Angeles, because he knew that Jennifer loved it. My guy liked holidays. Amusing, but also bittersweet, because I think he was trying to keep a connection to his parents by keeping up their traditions as the parent-figure for his sister.

He met my parents and got a stamp of approval that he didn't need to get, but I was glad to have anyway.

For Christmas, I gave him pictures, framed in silver, lots of them, of us, of him with his sister, Of the memories we were making. He put them next to his freshman yearbook, which now had a place of honor.

He gave me a Tiffany silver necklace with a diamond "S" on it for Sabrina, saying "you'll always be her mom." With this, if he wasn't there before, he cemented himself permanently in my heart. I wore it every day.

After the holidays, I visited my therapist.

"How are you feeling these days, Amelia?" asked Christian Gray.

I let out a deep breath.

"I am feeling so much better," I answered. "Truly. It's amazing. You know, when I was depressed, I didn't know it at first. It snuck up on me and I didn't realize that I was suffering. I was just numb. But then, after a while, with the treatment, with the medication, and with a whole lot of support, I started wanting to get out of bed every day. I started wanting to feel things. I wanted to smell the ocean, enjoy drinking good coffee, get mad, get angry, stand up for myself, and, for God's sake, feel sexy. It's a little embarrassing to admit, but I think that your advice to 'feel sexy' was the best advice that I could have ever received."

She smiled, a warm, gentle smile. And a little knowing.

I continued. "It matters how I feel about myself. It matters what I think about my body. And it matters that I feel comfortable in it, that I feel like it is okay to, I don't know, *inhabit* my body."

"That's absolutely right," she agreed. "This is progress. Well done."

"And you know, I think that the orgasms helped," I giggled.

"Of course they did," she laughed.

"Seriously," I went on. "I think they altered my brain chemistry. I think that the depression was an imbalance in there somehow, and getting in the good stuff, the pleasure, helped."

She nodded.

"Falling in love helped, too," I continued shyly.

"How is Ryan these days?" she asked.

"He's amazing," I answered. "He is a rock. I think that because of his past, because he lost his parents so young, and had to work through those issues, and take care of his sister, all the while being just eighteen or nineteen or twenty, meant that he grew up. Plus having to deal with having money all of a sudden and all of these people asking him for things. He is just solid. I couldn't have tethered my recovery to a better anchor."

She smiled.

"He also just accepts me as I am," I said quietly. "He doesn't try to change me. Sometimes he gets pissed at me, but he always tells me. He doesn't play games. He just loves me. And I love him."

She nodded. "I am happy to hear that your relationship is going well. How do you feel about your communication with him?"

"It's great. He knows all of my secrets. And I mean all of them. And he challenges me, he laughs with me. Half the time, I really can't believe he's real. He tells me what he's thinking, what he's doing with his business, what he thinks about the future."

"Do you ever fight?"

"Sure, we have. I got mad the other day and let him have it and he gave it right back. But I feel like we can work through it. I guess I just feel *healthy*."

"It sounds like it."

"So now at work, I'm still stressed about this case I'm working on," I continued, telling her about how Jake wanted me to do a case that I didn't think was good for my career, but would be good for his.

Having someone to talk things over with, was so unbelievably wonderful. My therapist was a key to my recovery: having the ability to unburden myself every week of my troubles, and being able to look at them from a distance, really mattered.

Ryan was a major source of my recovery too. My Sun God. My gorgeous, loving, beautiful man.

But the real part of my recovery was me. I was the one who was enough. I was the one who was no longer fucked up inside—or at least not as fucked up as I was before. We're all fucked up inside to some degree. But you could get past it. You could feel good about yourself, and feel all of the feelings, the good and the bad, and let it be.

Having friends, a partner, a professional, and others to help made it all worthwhile. I couldn't wait to see what the next adventure would be.

Two months later.

I was driving down Highway 101 with Ryan in my convertible. The top was down and the wind was blowing through our hair. Even though it was late January, it was unseasonably warm. California, my friends. These days, I found myself not caring if my hair was mussed. I wanted to feel the air, smell the ocean, and taste its salt, even in the daylight.

We were headed back from a dinner in Santa Barbara and going to Ryan's house for the night.

Oh, and I must brag about something. At dinner, I was accosted by yet another fucking blonde bitch warning me off of Ryan. I know, ridiculous, right? But this time, I was sober and prepared to launch a counter-attack. Before she finished the "I can't believe you're with Ryan Fielding" speech, I interrupted her, gave her The Hand, and said, "I don't know who you are or why you think you can judge him or me. You can't. He is the most sincere person I have ever met. He's proved it over and over again to me. He doesn't have to do it to you."

And with that, I flounced away, pleased with myself for finally sticking up for myself and for what I knew to be true about Ryan.

So we drove to his house, listening to Marie's Wild Child CD, which I still needed to return to her, the last part of that last song, "The Tale of You and Me" came on, the part where it changed tempo from the dark lyrics to the message of hope, and everyone sang together that it really was going to be alright—we'd make it so.

EPILOGUE

Full Circle

Six Months Later

H E WAS THRUSTING INTO ME FROM behind, his sweat dripping on my back, veins straining in his brawny forearms that clutched my pale, naked hips.

I was so fucking into this, I could hardly breathe. But I let out a moan and it was a real, honest-to-fuck moan. I couldn't keep my reactions away from Ryan, and I never needed to fake anything with him. And because he was always completely focused, completely into fucking me thoroughly, and enjoying my reaction, he always knew when to push it, and when to take it easy on me.

I guess today was a day to push it, because the next thing I knew, he surprised me by pulling his cock out, and smacked me hard on my ass.

I gasped.

Ryan had never spanked me before. I had never been spanked before, by anyone.

But fuck me, I liked it. What a surprise. It was just a little bite, then he thrust into me again, hitting the exact right spot on the front of my pussy, which really wanted to let go and visit the land of orgasm. I was ready to climax. But no, then he pulled out, again, and smacked me on the other side of my ass.

Fuck.

Thrust. Withdraw. Smack. Thrust. Withdraw. Smack.

I was wet and it was wild.

He kept up this crazy rhythm of pummeling me with his cock and spanking me on different parts of my ass. With every thrust, with every spank, my breasts jolted forward, my pussy clenched, and oh, my, he was wearing me out.

So, my Sun God was back and in full form.

And he was hotter than ever.

I guess I had come full circle. Before, I was worried about getting an orgasm, any orgasm, even a little one. Now, my guy had coaxed out of me so many reliable orgasms, and fuck me, multiple most of the time, that he was now experimenting with drawing it out, making me wait, denying me orgasms. Such delicious torture.

Bastard.

Good thing that I loved him.

And my body loved this. I loved the way our bodies moved together. I loved his combination of hard and gentle. I loved his attention to me. I loved the connection of our bodies, and the sensations that I felt in my body, in my brain, and in my heart.

I couldn't wait for the flood of the good shit in my brain that comes when you come. Since that day in the storage room in Southwinds, I had been counting on consistent, and awesome, sex as part of my recovery from depression. It really worked.

But right now?

"Ryan, you bastard, let me come now or I'll do it myself," I yell-whispered at him.

"Whatever you say," he muttered in my ear, and he thrust in and stayed there, not moving, bringing two hands (two!) to stimulate my clit, and the combination of him rubbing my wet clit and pressing his long, exquisite cock into my g-spot meant virtually instant orgasm for me.

Yay!

My body took over, shaking involuntarily, as he rode it out of me, my torso shuddering, impaled on his cock. And then my shaking and shuddering apparently set off his orgasm, as he groaned and bit my neck, pressing his cock up super high into my pussy as he came in a rush of warm spurts.

And then he collapsed, pushing me down onto the bed, so that I collapsed too, and he covered me completely with his big, warm, tan body. He propped himself up with his elbows so he wasn't squishing me too badly, and sucked my ear.

Then he pulled out, rolled to his back, rolled me under his arm, and let out a breath. I snuggled into his nook, biting the muscle over his armpit. I had a particular fondness for this piece of manmeat on him.

There's another word, manmeat.

Focus.

But fuck, that part of him was so good-looking, with a muscle stretching from his arm to his shoulder, that I had to nibble it. He had told me that it was strangely erotic for him when I nibbled there. Therefore, I did it, and often.

So.

To update.

We were on vacation in his beach house in Hawaii, in an area north of the Kona airport.

Yeah, I was suffering. Not at all.

After some discussion, a few months ago, we both got tested, both came out clean, so there had been no condoms for us for quite a while. I had been on the pill anyway, and it felt unbelievable to have him in me, no latex, just him. Apparently he agreed, by the filthy, contented words that came out of his mouth as he slid in. But now I was the one to clean up afterward, not him. Oh well. It felt good.

We spent a lot of time with each other. We both had clothes at both houses, and traded off where we would spend the night. It depended on our schedules, but it seemed to work, at least for now.

We had coordinated taking a vacation together at Ryan's house north of Kona, because of course he had a beach house in Hawaii. It was not as big as his beach house in Ventura, but it was plenty comfortable, with three bedrooms, three bathrooms, and a porch that wrapped almost the whole way around the house. The furniture was pale and beachy and tough and could handle sand and surf. It was ocean-front, a white sand beach, with black lava rock surrounding it on the sides. When I took my first step in the water, I was pleasantly surprised to find that the water temperature was so warm and comfortable, matching the warmth of the air. Ryan's view included palm trees dotting the landscape, scented plumeria flowers, and hibiscus everywhere. It was paradise.

That evening, after we cleaned up and I put on a tank top and a sarong, Ryan grilled a pizza for me on his outdoor grill.

A few things to note about this.

First, and most important, Ryan grilled shirtless. He wore red surfer trunks, tied in the front with white string, which hung down low on his hips, so hello happy trail and hello hip bones. This, plus shirtless Ryan equaled V-sighting. Not to mention the whole cornucopia of torso muscles. And have I gone into details about his back? My God.

Do you know how distracting it was for Ryan to cook for you shirtless, outside, in paradise in Hawaii? I may or may not have distracted him on his porch, out in the open, although his house was secluded, on my knees, because he deserved it. He may or may not have needed a sign of my appreciation of the floor show. This may or may not have delayed dinner a bit, but neither of us minded.

Second, Ryan was grilling pizza. I didn't know you could grill pizza. Pizza previously had been in the realm of good pizza and bad pizza, but either way it came out of an oven. But now? I don't know how my surfer learned these things, but he grilled the homemade dough first on both sides, and then added cheese and fresh toppings, grilled it a little longer so that the cheese melted, and served it. So, while I knew that such a thing as bad pizza existed, it didn't exist for me anymore.

Just like bad sex. It didn't exist for me anymore.

Accio orgasm!

And in the months that we had been together, I started paying attention to what Ryan did and how he acted and I realized that I was totally off base for believing anything anyone said about him being insincere or cheating. He just wasn't. We talked about it again, and the deal was that before me, he just wasn't seriously dating anyone, and they all really wanted him to be seriously dating them because he was amazing. (He didn't say this last part, I just filled in the blanks.)

But he was devoted to me, and I was devoted to him. He made my heart beat faster, and he accepted me, just as I was, with my insecurities and faults and flaws and messed up parts. He also made me feel like I was beautiful, like I was smart, and like I was funny. He laughed at me and then looked at me like he was going to devour me.

And sometimes he did.

The next day, south of Kailua-Kona, Hawaii

"Hold out your hand."

Ryan placed a green coffee berry in my hand. He kept one for himself and started to tear into it, then showed me the detritus in his hand.

"See, this? This pale thing is the coffee bean. They dry them here, and then ship them to me where I roast them for Southwinds."

We were exploring one of the small coffee farms above the highway that Ryan contracted with to supply him with coffee for Southwinds. I learned that they started picking coffee first at the lower elevations, and then moved their way up the hills. I also received a lecture about the entire process of growing and harvesting coffee beans, which was fascinating. To think that I was so addicted to this stuff, and it came from little farms, just like this one. He was in his element, chattering to the farmers, asking questions about growing conditions and farming issues, and holding my hand the entire time.

Later

"Fuck yeah, baby, that's it. That's it. It's coming. It's coming. Okay, now paddle, paddle, paddle."

I lay on a surfboard in the warm Hawaiian water, wearing a long-sleeve, rash guard shirt, and bikini bottoms, lying on my belly, my toes sticking into the water, my arms paddling as fast as I could.

Suddenly, I felt it. The wave picked me up and, with a surge of ocean energy, propelled me forward.

I was surfing! I was catching a wave!

Okay, but now I needed to stand up.

I awkwardly scrambled to my feet, and sort of made it up, staying standing for a few seconds, before I fell off backwards into the clear ocean.

Sputtering, I came up, but I was stoked. I had caught a wave!

The leash around my ankle holding the surfboard tugged me, and I reached down and grabbed it, pulling the board to me.

Ryan caught the next wave, expertly stopped by me, hopped off his board, and helped me up.

"You did it, Movie Star. Fucking awesome. Want to do it again?"

"Abso-fucking-lutely," I said.

Last day of our vacation

We walked hand in hand along the shore, and then stopped, our toes in the warm water, watching the sky change from blue to purple to pink to bright fuchsia with red and orange and yellow mixed in. I wore a dark purple bikini top, and a purple print sarong, with a white hibiscus flower in my dark hair, Ryan wore green Hawaiian print trunks and no shirt because I forbade him from wearing one.

"Watch for it," Ryan ordered, as the sun moved down into the ocean horizon. The sun went from full sun to a half-circle to a blip at the edge, to, yes! the green flash.

It wasn't just a myth. There was a flash of green light as the sun went down and the moon came up.

The water lapped at our feet, buried in the white sand.

A flock of water birds flew in formation, low along the shore.

Sailboats cruised by quietly, heading back to the harbor for the evening.

The pink, white, and yellow plumeria scented the air.

It was just us, on a deserted beach.

Then.

Ryan reached into the waistband of his trunks, in one of those little inner mesh pockets, and pulled out a diamond ring the size of an ice rink.

He got down on both knees in front of me.

My heart seized up and he started talking.

"I love you and you love me. You are the only one I have ever loved. I want to be with you for the rest of my life and I want to make it official. Marry me, Amelia," he said, green eyes sparkling.

Well.

Oh my. My stomach dropped and my heart beat faster. But the thing was, there was no question. Absolutely. No question about it. The rest of my life with my own personal Sun God? I couldn't think of anything better. I was so in love with him, I risked diving into schmaltz to tell you about it.

But I couldn't resist getting in a little sass.

"Are you asking me or telling me?"

"Both."

I smiled, looked at him with my cool, violet eyes to his warm, green ones, and said "Yes."

BONUS

In the coffee shop, first meeting

I LOOKED UP TO SERVE THE NEXT person in line and locked eyes with a violet pair that I'd recognize anywhere.

Holy fuck.

Amelia Crowley. My wet dream.

Amelia Crowley, prom queen. Amelia Crowley, senior class president. Amelia Crowley, Harvard-bound.

Fuck.

I looked at her. Glossy dark mane of hair. Technicolor eyes. She was hot. H.O.T. All Bond girl hot, with a suit racing around her beautiful curves. Intelligent hot. Beautiful hot. She was my centerfold. My ideal. Shit.

And she walked into Southwinds, looking like a movie star. A full on pinup.

She could be mine now.

I hadn't thought about her in years but it all came rushing back to me. The hottest girl in high school. The only one I had ever wanted. The one I dreamed of if I thought of my dream girl. She never looked at me in high school, but I was a freshman when she was a senior. And none of the shit had happened to me yet.

More than ten years later, I've grown up. And, it looked like, so did she. In all the right places.

She breathed out and words came out of those lush, full lips as she gave me her order.

And I was hard.

It was like I hadn't left high school and couldn't control my dick. Unbelievable.

I rung her up and took her card to swipe it. Same last name. I looked at her hand. No ring.

Game on.

I prayed for my pants to behave. Down boy. It wasn't the time.

As I handed her card back to her, she touched me. There was, honest to God, fucking electricity.

It was time to come up with a plan.

I put my nose back to the grindstone (or in this case, my straining dick to the counter, hoping to hide it) and handled the next person in line, the whole time aware of nothing but Amelia, standing off to the side.

She didn't recognize me, but I didn't care. I was going after her. She was going to be mine.

After the kiss in the surfside parking lot

I pulled my grandfather's 1968 Ford F-100 truck into my garage and closed the door.

Amelia Fucking Crowley. She still looked like a movie star.

I kissed her. I had wanted to do that for what, ten years? More? She tasted like Mexican food and hot girl. I had to see her again.

No. I needed to fuck her.

I headed out of the garage into my house and went straight to the shower to wash off the ocean water and salt.

I stripped off my clothes and turned on the water, waiting for it to warm up. It didn't take long and I stepped in, dipping my head to get my out-of-control hair wet, my muscles relaxed.

The warm water pounded my skin and I soaped up, washing my body clean, but my thoughts were anything but. Her eyes. Those gorgeous, violet blue eyes. That hair. I wanted to weave my hands in her hair. That body.

Yeah, that body. Fuck me, a body made for guys to worship.

Nipped in waist. Amelia's curvy, hot hips and ass. Gorgeous legs. Soft skin. Soft breasts. Soft hair.

Soft to my hard.

She turned me on without even knowing that she was doing it.

Fuck.

As my hand found my dick, I stroked it, soft at first, and then harder and faster, pumping myself. I wanted Amelia in my bed and I wanted her in *her* bed. I wanted to fuck her until she moaned my name, and then screamed for mercy. I wanted to feel her shuddering beneath me. I wanted to give her pleasure she had never known before. I wanted to lick her soft skin, eat her pussy, and inhale her scent. I wanted to get to know her breasts on a first-name basis. I wanted to talk dirty to her until she couldn't take it anymore. I wanted her up against the wall, in my truck, on the beach, at night, in the morning, and every way I could have her.

I closed my eyes and moved my hand faster and faster, gripping with more tension, feeling the vein in the underside of my dick come alive, feeling the tip straining, feeling my balls pulling up, the pressure mounting, until I came with a groan, pulsing and shuddering, wet spurts hitting the walls of my shower, thinking, always, of her.

Before the company dinner

The next customer set down a yogurt on the counter and ordered a latte. Amelia's order.

I thought about her smoking hot body, her lacy thong between the globes of her gorgeous ass, her tiny waist, and her face.

Shit.

My dick stirred.

Thinking of her would get me into trouble at work. I didn't need the distraction. It didn't help that I could still taste her on my lips.

After the Fielding Pharmaceuticals Foundation dinner

A drunk Amelia is a fucking funny Amelia.

Total dream come true to have her with me at the dinner tonight, setting aside her freak-out sessions. Total. Fucking. Dream. Come. True.

And her freak-outs showed me a secret part of her. I was going to get through to her and she was going to be mine.

In every way.

I felt bad for all that had happened to her. I wanted her to be happy. Not freaked out. I wanted to protect her, although I know full well you can't protect someone from shit that already happened. I was going to try anyway.

The more I learned about her the more I liked her. The more I thought she was strong and beautiful.

Ironic to think that the more she learned about me, the more she got pissed at me. I mean, she got pissed at me because she didn't know that I was more than just a coffee shop slacker-surfer.

Not cool.

I got over it pretty fast, though. She seemed to not care either way and was just surprised to find out. I figured she knew.

But fuck, if she was going to get pissed, the makeup sex was hot. I had to remember that.

Something else was bothering her tonight, though. I was going to have to find out what it was.

I decided to take her home and let the suite at Bacara go—I wanted some privacy tonight and, honestly, I wanted to see her in my bed, at my beach house, that gorgeous body all spread out for me in the moonlight.

So since I was a horny son of a bitch, I'd tell you: I wanted her naked, spread out, glistening bare pussy and full, perfect globes of her tits ready for me. I wanted to run my tongue down her body, lick her belly button, and kiss her ribs. I wanted to make her aroused, smell her turn on, and get her pussy all plump and wet and creamy. And I wanted her specifically in my house, by the beach, with all of the windows open, the waves crashing outside, the moonlight on the water and reflecting on her skin, the moist air.

And that was just for starters.

That had pretty much been my fantasy every night for the past few weeks—at least the nights that I was not with her. Horny bastard here wanted to see what it was like for real.

I already had a taste of it in her bed. I swear, I couldn't believe the way she looked the first time I had her in her bed. All that beauty. Hot freaking girl. Mine.

She thought she owned her sexuality with her rules, but the truth was, *she had no idea*. She was so wrong. I was going to teach her to own her sexuality. By the time I taught her to open up, she was going to just own it. *Own it.*

And, hopefully, share it with me.

I would admit it: She was the best I ever had. It was amazing that with all the shit in her history, she was so hot—once she opened up—so responsive, so fucking turned on.

She aroused me.

All night long.

Truthfully, she aroused me for most of the past few weeks.

Yeah, I was a horny fucker.

Tonight, man, tonight was almost too much to take.

Jen, my little sister, was still at school so I had to go tonight to represent the family. But I was glad that I went even if I had no choice, and even though the event always brought up a lot of bad memories about my parents' deaths, and even though tonight there was drama for Amelia.

Because this time my Movie Star was with me.

In past years, I just took one of the society blondes, like Tiffany or Ashley or Destiny or Taylor, because I needed to take someone and they were good for a quick fuck, and looked good in the pictures, but they didn't mean anything.

Not like Amelia.

No one else meant anything.

A guy's gotta find it somewhere, but when a woman was the whole package—brains, beauty, attitude—fuck. I didn't want anyone else. I know it was a cliché, but I had eyes only for her. True story.

She was so hot tonight all dressed up. That face. That dress. That body. So fucking lush. She was like a feast. She didn't need to do anything to make me want her.

But then she started drinking the wine (there were two open bottles on each table and they kept getting replenished) and the night got more interesting.

She hissed like she was in a fucking vaudeville audience when her ex walked past. He didn't acknowledge her. That was a good thing. I would have had to kick his ass if he said any shit to her and that was a bad idea at the Fielding Pharmaceuticals Foundation annual charity dinner. Especially a bad idea if the oldest Fielding was the one to deliver the ass-kicking.

She was polite during the speeches and had the biggest smile on her face when I got up there to thank everyone for coming and to tell them to pull out their wallets and empty them out for cancer research.

But while the keynote speaker gave her speech and the President of the Board of Directors of the Foundation talked, she got closer and closer to me, her hand moving up my leg, resting at the top of my thigh, her mouth in my ear, whispering funnier than hell comments all night long. As she drank more and the night went on, she went from sweet to increasingly sexier and sexier—if that was even possible with her. I just tried to keep her drinking water in the meanwhile, which wasn't too hard to do. She wasn't a loud drunk, she was a fun drunk, and it was hotter than hell.

I have no idea how I walked out of there, my dick was so painful.

I caught her when she came back from the bathroom. I didn't know what happened, she had her fist up, and she seemed to have gotten into a fight, but she was in no condition to tell me. She seemed okay, though. After dinner was done, Amelia was D-O-N-E. She giggled and held on to me to walk. She was totally adorable. She smelled amazing.

I got her in the car and drove us to my house.

When we got there, I pulled the Tesla into my garage and parked it between the 4-Runner and the McLaren. (A 650s Spider, black, if you were wondering.) It was a quiet ride home since she fell asleep after telling me how, exactly, she was going to suck my dick, even though (she told me) she had never done it before and even though she said she wasn't going to do it again, she was going to do it one time just to break her rules.

Her sex rules were hilarious. Sex rules. I would show her some sex rules. Like, it was a rule that she must have multiple orgasms every time. Or, it was a rule that, like Russell Brand says, I was the second coming, always. Ladies first, you know.

I was not sure that she knew what she was saying in the car but it was still funnier than hell just the same. And the whole time, since she was a quiet drunk, she was whispering those dirty words. To me. All this sex coming out of her full lips. Fuck me. The hard-on would not go away.

I felt like a warning in an ad for Viagra. "If you have an erection lasting more than four hours … ."

Too bad she was in no condition to take care of it now.

Time to take my Bond girl hottie to bed.

I went around and opened up the car door and caught her as she slumped. She woke up a little, but I didn't trust her to walk. Not in those shoes. But there was no way I would tell her to take them off. I had amended my earlier fantasy to include her wearing nothing but those silver high heels in my bed.

Yeah.

I lifted her up and she put her head on my shoulder, cuddling against me.

God I loved that.

I kicked the car door closed, beeped it, and went into my beach house.

"You're so pretty," she murmured, and I laughed, quietly, but hard.

I walked to my bedroom and set her on my bed. It was a full moon night, an autumn moon, and the night was clear. I opened up the sliding glass doors and let the salty, moist ocean air come in. I went back to the bed and unzipped her dress with the zipper located along her side. It wasn't easy, but I got her out of it and looked back at my handiwork.

Dark, curly brown hair splayed out across my white pillows. Pale shoulders. Arms spread out, long elegant fingers resting on the mattress. She was wearing just a sage green satin bra with no shoulder straps and matching teeny, satiny panties. And those silver shoes. Her legs went on and on.

Whoa.

My bed was a good place to be.

Too bad she was asleep. I looked forward to waking her up in the morning.

I carefully unhooked her bra and took off her shoes, even though I didn't want to. Okay, so I copped a little feel of her tits. But no more.

Then I got her a Yater board t-shirt of mine and put it on her. She helped a little.

Then I stripped and crawled in next to her, her cool skin next to my warm body, and cradled her all night long.

AUTHOR'S NOTE

As may be obvious from the subject matter of this book, I had my own personal journey through deep, suicidal depression. Years of essentially untreated depression led to a bad crisis in 2014. My personal recovery involved hospitalization, medication, therapy, exercise, saying no to things I didn't want to do, allowing myself to do the things that I really wanted to do (like writing), and being open about my story. I wanted you to know, if you are suffering from depression, that you are not alone. I came out of it, and you can too. If you need help, please get it. Depression is not your fault and you can get better. I'm rooting for you.

The National Suicide Prevention Lifeline in the United States is 1-800-273-8255 and www.suicidepreventionlifeline.org and there are local mental health resources everywhere.

I love you and I encourage you to get help. No question about it: it's worth it.

ABOUT THE AUTHOR

Leslie McAdam is a California girl who loves romance, Little Dude, and well-defined abs. She lives in a drafty, old farmhouse on a small orange tree farm in Southern California with her husband and two small children. Leslie always encourages her kids to be themselves—even if it means letting her daughter wear leopard print from head to toe. An avid reader from a young age, she will always trade watching TV for reading a book, unless it's Top Gear. Or football. Leslie is employed by day but spends her nights writing about the men you fantasize about. She's unapologetically sarcastic and notoriously terrible at comma placement.

Always up for a laugh, Leslie tries to see humor in all things. When she's not in the writing cave you'll find her fangirling over Beck, camping with her family, or mixing up oil paints to depict her love of outdoors on canvas.

Find her on Facebook at www.facebook.com/lesliemcadamauthor or on Twitter at www.twitter.com/lesliemcadam

Preview of The Stars in the Sky
Book 2 in the Giving You... series

Foul-mouthed, tattooed, vegan Marie Diaz-Austin accepted a summer internship on a ranch north of Santa Barbara to work with underprivileged and special needs kids. Will Thrash, the gorgeous, but conservative rancher, wants nothing to do with left-wing liberals like her.

Although they hate each other's politics, they cannot deny their immediate and growing attraction to each other. What will give? Their principles or themselves?

A book about our ideologies and our human-ness. Politics and sex. Prejudices and beliefs.

CHAPTER 1: FIRST IMPRESSIONS

GOD, I REALLY HAD TO PEE.

Only ten more minutes to go until I got there. *Come on, come on, come on.* I willed my car to go faster. I was out in the middle of nowhere and I really did not want to have to stop and find a bush. I squeezed my thighs together. Since it was a hot June day, and I was wearing denim short-shorts, this just made me sticky and sweaty. Not helping.

The "time of arrival" on my GPS app ticked down to nine more minutes.

I put my foot on the gas pedal. My car was an old Mercedes sedan that had been converted to bio-diesel, so I should probably call it the accelerator rather than the gas pedal. I was trying to cut down on my use of fossil fuels. My car was powered by leftover vegetable oil from Chinese restaurants. My car proudly advertised its alternative fuel source on the back window in big green lettering. It always smelled like kitchen grease wherever I went, but I would do anything for the environment.

This morning, before I had left my apartment for the summer, with my car packed up for this next big adventure, I stopped by the new Santa Barbara location of Southwinds coffee, the local coffee chain owned by the boyfriend of my best friend, Amelia Crowley. Amelia's fiancé, Ryan Fielding, happened to be working there when I stopped in, so I chatted with him while they made me the most amazing coffee. He knew that I was vegan, therefore I didn't even need to say that my coffee needed to have non-GMO soy milk and organic coffee beans. He just checked the boxes and handed it to the barista and then smiled at me and asked me about my summer internship.

Boy, he was cute. Yes, he was my best friend's surfer hottie, and they were totally devoted to each other, and I would never get in the way of that, but I had eyes and it was impossible not to stare. The fact that I was looking at him, however, probably meant that I seriously needed to get laid.

I shouldn't have ordered the ginormous soy latte, though.

Seven minutes to go. Now I was bouncing along a dirt road. The ruts and ribs in the road did nothing good for my bladder.

God, I didn't know if I could make it. I felt like a little kid. The bushes on the side of the road were starting to look mighty tempting.

I was driving to Headlands Ranch, my temporary home and job site for the summer. For the past year, I had been going to school at the University of California at Santa Barbara, getting an advanced degree in Counseling Psychology. I became interested in counseling, honestly, after being with Amelia when she went through her suicidal depression. I felt hamstrung by not knowing what to do to help her. So, I went back to school, keeping my job as a preschool teacher at a progressive school during the day, and going to school at night. Although I wasn't sure where I wanted to end up, either setting up my own practice, or working somewhere, I knew that I wanted to help disadvantaged or special needs youth.

Hence, my interest in a counseling job at Headlands.

I had found Headlands Ranch on the internet after I saw an internship posting on Craigslist. From its website, I learned that Headlands was run by the fourth generation of an old California farming family, with William Charles Thrash, III now in charge.

Headlands Ranch was located on California's Central Coast, about halfway between Los Angeles and San Francisco, north of Santa Barbara near Santa Ynez. This was a rural part of California, where gentle rolling hills met the Pacific Ocean. Often green with lush grass during winter rains (if we were lucky), the hills were brown in summer, with stocky, Coast Live Oak trees standing guard over row upon row of grapevines. It looked like the famous Napa Valley in parts, but it did not get as cold in winter as Napa. The flatter areas generally were planted with row crops—strawberries in coastal areas, colder crops like kale and cilantro inland. Some areas had cattle grazing; being a vegan, I did not approve of their ultimate use. But the area more than made up for it with its natural beauty. Only a few scattered towns were in this area, which had an overall tiny population compared to the urban areas of California.

While the ranch was a diversified farming operation, with apparently everything from organic strawberries to blueberries to avocados to citrus to grapes for wine, what interested me was its affiliated nonprofit association. Headlands Ranch ran a therapeutic horsemanship and agricultural program, called the Headlands

Program, which was my new employer.

It had two types of programs. The first was for urban kids from Los Angeles, San Francisco, and other cities in California such as San Jose, San Diego, and Sacramento. These were kids who had never seen a cow, and they essentially went to camp at Headlands for a week to experience new things: stay in a bunkhouse, learn to take care of animals, help around the ranch, and do teamwork skills. The other program was for special needs kids. The ranch had a lot of therapy horses and other animals, and the kids would come up and stay and spend time with the animals, learning to ride horses and spending time in the fresh air. With both programs, the kids would come up for a week with their adult leaders or parents, stay in a bunkhouse, help with easier tasks on the ranch, eat in a mess hall, and experience the rural life. The ranch received some grants for running this program, and it had had full-time horse wranglers and other staff. I was hired as a glorified camp counselor, to watch over the kids and help with any counseling that came up, as well as run the teamwork skills and games. I was lucky that it counted for internship credit for my graduate degree program.

This was going to be so much fun!

But not when I had a full bladder. As the clock on the GPS ticked down to five more minutes until arrival, I passed through a gate with an arch overhead that read HEADLANDS RANCH, ESTABLISHED 1910 in rustic font, very old-fashioned and Western-looking. I continued down a rolling dirt road and pulled up at a collection of farm buildings at the end of the line. There was a huge, old, white farmhouse, what looked like a bunk house, some newer looking ranch houses, a couple of barns, some corrals, and some other accessory buildings.

I parked my car and got out immediately, hoping against hope that there was a place to go pee, like, now.

A tall, thin, tan, no-nonsense, horsey-looking woman, forties-ish, with sea green eyes and long, straight blonde hair in a ponytail, came out of the bunkhouse and said, "You must be Marie Diaz-Austin. Welcome. I'm Janine Thompson, the head wrangler for the Headlands Program."

Sticking out my hand, I said, "It's nice to meet you. You wouldn't by any chance have a bathroom I could use, would you? It's been a long drive and I'm dying here."

She smiled warmly and pointed to the closest building, the old, white, farm house, and said, "Sure, go right ahead in there. Second door on the left down the hall."

I was embarrassed enough already, so I tried not to run, and instead walked really, really fast to the building, like they speed-walk in the Olympics, then ran up the stairs, flung open the front door, scooted down the hall at a clip, and opened the second door on the left—

—and literally ran, full body, full bore, into a naked, wet man, who staggered with the impact of my weight against him. My breasts hit his back, my legs straddled the sides of his, and I grabbed onto his soaking nude waist to keep from falling. The front of my shirt, my shorts, and my legs got wet from the water on him.

"The fuck?" he grunted.

"Ohmigod, I'm so sorry," I started as I jumped back immediately, hands up like I was being arrested, and then I got a look at him. He turned around to look at me, hands on hips, completely unabashed at wearing his birthday suit.

Well, this was interesting.

He was totally naked, as in just stepped out of the shower naked. He had not even had a chance to grab his towel, he was so naked. Did I mention that he was naked? And he was dripping on a bathmat, with the water that had not rubbed off on me running in rivulets to the ground, standing there, glaring at me.

I couldn't tell you what I noticed first about him, except that he was belongs-in-a-naughty-magazine's-centerfold attractive, so I'm just going to list what I saw, in body order, from top to toe.

He was really tall, like at least six inches taller than me, and I was a not-short five foot ten.

His hair was longish, wavy, wet (obviously), and a lush, dark brown.

The pair of eyes that glared at me were a deep, dark, chocolate brown. They were rimmed in enviable thick, dark brown lashes that curled. Why don't women ever get natural lashes like that?

His face was classically handsome, with strong eyebrows, a straight nose, and high cheekbones, with hollows underneath, and some yummy stubble along his square jaw.

He was tan everywhere. In other words, although this was a farm, he did not have a farmer tan. And, since he was naked (as I may have mentioned), I could tell. He had a brawny chest, strong, thick arms, with meaty forearms, a washboard waist, and strong legs.

And, his junk. Yep. There. Unlike a turtle, it was not hiding in a shell. He was at half staff and boy, full staff would be a treat. His junk was the kind of junk that you used "feet" rather than "inches" to measure. As in "more than half a foot," unerect. Well beyond.

A fucking gorgeous man.

Totally pissed at me.

I so knew how to make an entrance. I tried to salvage the situation, by mumbling "Janine told me I could use this bathroom," but he interrupted.

"Ever think of knocking?" he snarled, as he reached for a white towel and wrapped it around his waist, now looking like an ad for razor blades.

"I'm sorry," I said, aiming for sincerity. "It's been a long drive and I really have to pee." This last bit may have come out of my mouth just a wee bit desperately.

"Go down the hall, there's another bathroom. I'm using this one." And he pushed me out, by physically pushing my shoulders, and shut the door.

Way to start the interactions with my fellow staff.

I took off down the hall at a bit of a trot, found the bathroom, and relief. All was well, for now.

As I headed back down the hallway, his bathroom door opened and he came out, dressed in dark blue Wrangler jeans, with a huge belt and belt buckle, a tight, faded blue t-shirt, and cowboy boots, hair still messy, curly, and wet.

He looked me up and down and said, "You're a fucking liberal, aren't you?" Then he reached into his back pocket and pulled out a can of Copenhagen and stuffed some chew in his cheek.

Disgusting.

And, the fuck?

I was extremely liberal, but so what? How could he tell? I was wearing normal clothes: my denim short-shorts, Tom's shoes, and a white cami (that was probably see-through due to my literal run-in with Mr. Shower). I would have to change.

Well, I suppose my non-conservative status was obvious, given my tattoos and my eyebrow piercing. My hair was normally dyed in colors that were not found in nature. But right now, it was a bleached blonde, and would probably stay that way for the summer. Naturally, my hair was a medium brown, to match my medium brown eyes. I was skinny, with long legs (it was genetics, my parents were that way) but I had some boobage going on (again, genetics).

But how dare he judge me so quickly. And what do my politics have to do with working on a ranch?

"What's wrong with that?" I shot back.

"Darlin', life's too short to list all the things that are wrong with being a liberal," he drawled, and then sauntered out the front door and down the steps of the ranch house.

Oh, I was pissed at him for being such a gross, judgmental asshole. But I didn't want to get into a fight in the first five minutes of my new job so I kept my mouth shut. For now.

Still, I couldn't help but watch him go. He had a damn sexy walk, almost like he owned the land he was walking on. Now, I'm not one who goes for Wrangler jeans—my favorite type of music is "anything but country"—nevertheless I noticed that he filled them out well. But then he turned around and said, "This is Reagan Country, and don't forget it."

And he kept going until he was out of sight.

Reagan Country? Was he kidding? Was he even born during the Reagan years?

Ugh.

Motherfucker!

Made in the USA
San Bernardino, CA
03 May 2016